A Collection of Short Stories

Garnett Kilberg Cohen

Wiseblood Books

Milwaukee

Printed in the United States of America

Set in Arabic Typesetting

Cover by Dominic Heisdorf

While some of these stories may have been inspired by actual events, they are all works of fiction. The characters and incidents are the work of the author's imagination.

Library of Congress Cataloging-in-Publication Data

Cohen, Garnett Kilberg 1953— Swarm to

Glory/ Garnett Kilberg Cohen;

1. Cohen, Garnett Kilberg, 1953—fiction 2. Short Fiction

3. Women Writers   4. American Writers

ISBN-13: 978-1500219833

ISBN-10: 1500219835

TABLE OF CONTENTS

The following stories first appeared in the magazines listed:

"Swarm to Glory," *Crab Orchard Review*
"Bad News," *Michigan Quarterly Review*
      (Winner of the Lawrence Foundation Prize)
"Women with the Longest Hair," *Washington Square*
      (Special Mention, Pushcart Prize)
"The Fence," *The Pinch*
"Bottle of Wine," *Ontario Review*
"Thieves," *Pittsburgh Magazine*
"The Wedding Invitation," *Another Chicago Magazine*
"Triangulation," *The Roanoke Review*
"Casa Del Mar Azul," *Nebraska Review*

In addition to being grateful to the journals listed above, I wish to thank my husband, Fredric Cohen, for his love and support, and to thank friends, colleagues and family who provided encouragement and/or read and gave feedback on some of the stories in this collection, particularly, Vicky Anderson, Wendy Bartlo, Jody Becker, Rosellen Brown, Tsivia Cohen, JoAnn Connington, Ken Daley, Stuart Dybek, Sharon Evans, Kim Green, Maggie Kast, Jim Kilberg, Chuck Kinder, Karen Knowles, Sara Livingston, Andrew Medlrum, Cathy Mellett, Cilla Murray, Lynne Penczer, Jeanne Petrolle, Marni Rebmann, Susie Rosenthal, Matthew Shenoda, Elizabeth Shepherd, Peggy Shinner, Susan Sink, Lynn Sloan, Christine Sneed, Sharon Solwitz, and S.L. Wisenberg. I am indebted to Columbia College Chicago for its support and to all of the fine people at Wiseblood Books, particularly Joshua Hren and Charles Schmitt, for their talent, dedication and hard work.

From her lower bunk, Ellen could see two of her foster sisters, Berta and Polly. Both in worn pajamas, they clutched the windowsill, their noses pressed to the glass. Polly's pajamas had a design of pale pink strawberries. Berta's were printed with a nautical motif—sailboats, anchors, fish, and captains' wheels. They were both barefooted; their heels, creased and raw, faced the room. They stared out the window.

The morning sky was polka-dotted. Thick with moving spots.

"It's Armageddon," said Polly dully, tossing her long, rippling hair over a shoulder. When Ellen grew up, every time she saw a reproduction of Botticelli's Venus in a Half Shell, she would be reminded of how Polly's hair had amazed her.

"The end of days! The sky is falling!" cried Berta.

Her cries were infectious; Polly's screams joined her sister's. Both girls jumped up and down, flashing the pink soles of their feet. "The sky is falling—breaking into pieces! The Apocalypse."

❖

Berta and Polly were real sisters. The Freeman sisters. But Berta didn't have long hair. When she first arrived at the Wickles, it was so short and patchy that there were even some bald spots, a few crusty and brown with scabs. The haircut was connected to the reason their mother lost them to the state. But Ellen wasn't allowed to ask about the specific connection. It seemed silly to lose your children over a haircut. Ellen's mother was really sick—

very sick. In a hospital with special name. Ellen felt superior to the Freeman girls. She had a real reason to be in foster care.

Ellen sat up and tossed back her sheets. She stamped over to the window, spread her foster sisters apart to stand between them, and looked out the glass over the patio and the round septic tank beside it to the solitary tree in the center of the yard. The polka dots were moving, heading for the tree, clustering around it.

"They're not pieces of the sky, silly," said Ellen. "Look, they have wings. They're moving."

"Maybe they're angels. Little tiny baby angels?" asked Berta hopefully. Her hair was beginning to grow out; it resembled a large blonde clown wig. "Coming down to take us up to heaven."

"Them's bees, stupid," said Walter Wickle, bursting into the room. Walter Dill Pickle, they called him at school. And it was true; his skin had a greenish cast to it. Ellen was glad she hadn't been forced to take the Wickles' last name the way Walter had. Of course, they said it was the children's own decision, but the children knew the Wickles had subtle methods of coercion. Nancy Wickle said Mama Jean Wickle promised to give her an allowance if she changed her name. Nancy didn't care. She changed her name, saying that as long as the Wickles didn't adopt her, she was free to change her name back to the original after she turned eighteen. And the Wickles would never adopt anyone, Nancy said, since that would mean forfeiting the monthly support money from the state.

Besides Billy, Walter was the only boy in residence. Billy was really scary. Small for his age and wiry, he had an evil squint to his eyes. He bragged that his father was in prison. Walter wasn't naturally mean; he just tried to appear tough, but wasn't very convincing.

"Could you keep it down, pleeeeassse," mumbled Nancy from her top bunk. "It's not even seven a.m. yet."

Nancy always slept with the wristwatch her boyfriend, Hoagie, gave her, even though a white alarm clock with a glowing peach-colored light stood on top of the highest dresser where all four of them could see it.

"The yard is filled with bees," said Berta.

"What?" asked Nancy, throwing her long womanly legs over the edge of the bed. At sixteen, Nancy had lived with the Wickles the longest, ever since she was six-years-old. Even though Nancy was Ellen's favorite foster sister, sometimes Nancy's existence made Ellen nervous. Mrs. Hopper, Ellen's social worker, had said that foster care was only "a temporary measure," but Nancy's presence was living proof that the opposite might be true.

Nancy plopped down from her loft, flat on her feet. (In spite of Mama Jean Wickle's clucks of disapproval, Nancy wore nothing but an over-sized t-shirt to bed.) Nancy walked to stand behind the three younger children and stare over their heads.

"Hot damn! Those are bees!" said Nancy.

"Don't swear unless you want the angel of the Lord to come down and strike you dead," said Polly. Now that her screams had subsided, her voice had returned to its usual monotone.

"Shut up, knucklehead," said Walter.

"My, my, what's all this commotion?" said Mama Jean Wickle, her huge form slowly filling the doorway like a ship coasting to stop beneath a bridge. "Why to see y'all up so early, one would guess y'all looking forward to Sunday school. Now that would be a nice surprise."

"Oh my!" She gasped as she caught the sight out the window. "We'll have to talk to Ralph Lender, down at the church. Get him over here. He's a bee keeper."

❖

For the first three weeks her mother was in the hospital, Ellen lived with her mother's best friend, Paige. But Paige's husband wasn't accustomed to children, so after futile attempts to locate Ellen's father in South America (her parents divorced when Ellen was a baby), she was placed in foster care. Ellen could still remember the discomfort she felt when she first arrived at the Wickles, gripping the pink suitcase her mother used to let her pack all by herself when they went on vacations. Her social worker, Mrs. Hopper, carried the cardboard box containing Ellen's books and other belongings too large for the valise. Nancy was the only other foster girl staying with the Wickles at the time. She was kind to Ellen, took her in the bedroom, gave her the bunk beneath her own, and helped Ellen put her clothing away in the three drawers assigned to her in the smaller of the two dressers. The drawers were labeled, ELLEN GOLDBERG, with masking tape printed in black magic marker.

Afterward Nancy took her in the backyard to show her the hens and cocks. Some were white, some cinnamon colored. Ellen loved their brilliant red wattles and crowns. Ellen had never seen such creatures outside a petting zoo. She was pleased that a place where she would be staying had exotic animals roaming around as freely as cats.

The Wickles lived on a peculiar street, a rural route between Akron and Cleveland. In the early fifties, a farmer had sold it for development. Three split-levels were built before the construction company went broke. The Wickles bought one of the houses below cost. It had three bedrooms upstairs and a single big one in the split-level basement that opened right onto the cracked concrete patio next to the septic tank. The foster girls and the Wickles slept in two of the upstairs bedrooms. The boys slept in the basement. The girls' room had two bunk beds and two mismatched dressers. The third upstairs bedroom was used as a sewing and guestroom, though Ellen never saw an overnight visitor. And no one except Nancy (who wasn't allowed in the room) sewed. Mama Jean Wickle's grown son, her only natural child, Jack, a bachelor who worked for the sheriff's department, bought one of the other split-levels on the street. Construction on the third house was never finished. The place stood empty with boarded-over windows. The children were under strict orders not to go near it.

Long and winding, the rest of the road was spotted with trailers, shacks, and the original farmhouse where an old farmer still lived. All the structures were on one side of the road; the other side was an over-grown field of brambles and thistles, rabbits, other strange wildlife, and, according to Walter, snakes. Lots of people deposited their junk in the field, even a few old car shells, despite a huge NO DUMPING sign. The rural route was over ten miles long, bordered on both ends with commercial strips of motels, fast food restaurants, car dealers, and the like.

Except for school and church, Ellen seldom ventured farther than a mile in either direction of the Wickles' house, so she felt like they were deep in the country. She could hear crickets and frogs all night in the summer. Once in the morning, a gigantic pink and white mouse was flattened in the road. Mama Jean Wickle's husband, Harold, called it a 'possum. At first, Ellen thought he said it was a posing, and she wondered how anything so flat could be pretending to be dead.

Right after Ellen's mother went into the hospital, when she lived with Paige, Ellen visited her mother a few times a week. But the Wickles didn't want to drive all the way into Akron. It took a special call from the social worker's supervisor to prompt them. Harold Wickle took Ellen in his red Ford pick-up.

"We don't usually do this, you know," said Harold. "The parents are 'posed to come see you children, but seeing your mama is so sick, we made a 'ception in your case."

The Wickles didn't speak like Ellen's mother's friends. It was as if they didn't know all words in their entirety. Ellen never corrected them. She knew her mother would consider such an action impolite. Ellen was slightly embarrassed when Harold Wickle walked her to her mother's hospital room. He didn't dress like the other visitors—in slacks and shirts. He wore bib overalls. Even though he worked the line at Firestone Tires, he liked to pretend he was a farmer on Saturdays. Out at the rear of the yard, he had built a small barn and chicken shed; behind them was a huge vegetable garden. Billy said that was the reason the Wickles took in foster children—to slave in the garden. Since she had only been made to work in the garden a few times, Ellen thought he had invented the story to frighten her.

During that visit to the hospital, Ellen was stunned to see her mother's transformation. A perpetual dieter, always five or ten pounds overweight, her mother was a tangle of bones. Her wrists were so thin that Ellen (against her wishes) imagined snapping them over her knee. Her mother's eyes were sunken, ringed in black. Her head didn't even make a dent in the hospital foam pillow. After that, Ellen didn't ask to go visit her mother again. She preferred to speak to her by phone, that way, on good days, when her mother's voice wasn't too raspy, Ellen could imagine her the way she used to look.

Ellen didn't even see her mother on her tenth birthday. She didn't tell the Wickles it was her birthday; Ellen didn't want Mama Jean Wickle to bake a cake, as if she was just like the other foster children. The lack of acknowledgment allowed her to keep the world where she and her mother lived—the world in her head—more real than the Wickle household.

❖

By the time the foster children were dressed for church, the bees clung in a solid ball around the tree branches, looking like an apple on a stick or a Tootsie Pop tree with buzzing leaves.

Mama Jean Wickle shepherded all the children out through the side door, under the bright green, corrugated plastic roof of the carport. They were instructed to file quickly into the vehicles, without even glancing in the backyard.

"Don't look—y'all don't want no stinger in your eye," said Mama Jean Wickle, her palm in the small of Ellen's back as she led her into the car. Mama Jean Wickle was a tall woman with frizzy yellow hair. The far side of obese, she was the type of fat that made the front part of her body seem to swing into a place just slightly before her rear end. "Ralph Lender will take care of them right after church. He'll get them bees to high tail out of that tree."

The church the Wickles belonged to was a strange building, big and round and low, like an extra large flying saucer that had landed right on the edge of Akron. Even the name, the Cathedral of Tomorrow, made Ellen think of science fiction movies and space ships and interplanetary travel.

The roof of the building was dome shaped. On Ellen's first visit, the preacher, Reverend Rex Humbard, was collecting money to have the dome painted gold. Ellen's mother and her friends were always raising money for things like starving children in Africa and political prisoners in South America. Ellen had never heard of such a thing as donating money to paint a roof gold. But Reverend Rex Humbard seemed to be having much better luck than her mother. People were falling all over each other to bestow dollars for the roof.

Ellen and her mother didn't attend church. Her mother had told Ellen that God wasn't a person or a supernatural being. Her mother claimed that the lord resided in all things: the birds and the bees, the flowers and the trees, even inside Ellen herself. Yet sometimes Ellen visited churches with her friends. Those buildings—Methodist, Episcopal, and Lutheran—seemed stern places where you sat on hard benches and tried not to cough or move. The ministers talked about God as if he were an intolerant man. The Cathedral of Tomorrow was nothing like those places. It was more like the Grand Ole Opry that Mama, Jean Wickle and her husband, Harold, watched on television.

14

The seating area was as spacious as the auditorium where Ellen's mother had taken her to see The Mikado in Cleveland. Each worshiper had his or her own movie-theater-like chair with a plush red velvet slipcover that matched the curtains on stage. People came and went from their seats as they pleased. And Reverend Rex's God sounded like a king in a fairy tale. Ellen imagined him sitting in a golden throne, surrounded by billowing clouds and angels, checking with Rex to see who should be admitted to Heaven and who should be turned away. And Rex talked about Jesus even more than he did about God.

In between Rex's preaching and collecting, trios of gospel singers with high blond bouffant hairstyles sang. Sometimes Reverend Rex's wife sang solos. She usually wore a shimmering evening gown.

The church-theater was in the center of the building, like the bulls-eye of a target, the next ring was a wide hallway, and around that was an outer circle of offices, restrooms, and storage rooms. Since the sermons were all telecast around the northern Ohio area, there was a lot of equipment—cameras, microphones, and the like—to store.

On her first trip to the Cathedral of Tomorrow, Ellen didn't have to go to Sunday school. She just listened to the sermon about the golden roof and walked around the wide hallway— the family promenading in their Sunday best—being introduced by Mama Jean Wickle. Almost everyone she met said the same thing:

"Not another one, Jean! Praise Jesus! Why you have a heart of gold! The Lord needs more generous women like you."

"I'm just doing my Christian duty," she would answer, beaming all the same. To a few people, Mama Jean Wickle whispered something when she thought Ellen wasn't listening. But Ellen heard.

This one's a Jew.

Sometimes the listener gasped in response, then stared at Ellen as if she might take off in flight. But once, an ugly weasel like man with a pock marked face said, "I wouldn't let none of that kind into my house."

Mama Jean Wickle acted a little huffy in response. Ellen pretended to be counting pennies in her pink vinyl purse.

"Well, it might be true that salt and pepper belong in their own separate shakers," said Mama Jean Wickle. "But I'll stomach a strange spice if it means I have the chance to introduce one child to Jesus Christ."

Ellen had no idea why Mama Jean was talking about pepper and salt shakers—though she thought the "strange spice" part might have something to do with the hospital where her mother was staying. Wasn't spice in the name?

"Jesus, hisself, was a Jew once," said the weasel-man's wife, obviously trying to atone for her husband's rudeness.

"That is correct," said Mama Jean Wickle nodding her head rapidly in approval, as if it was a fact few people knew, and she was delighted that the woman had pointed it out to her ignorant husband.

After that first visit Ellen was often allowed to wander in and out of the main church as she liked once Sunday School ended. The special promenades were reserved, Ellen learned, for the first Sundays of new foster children. Usually Ellen sat through the singers and the beginning of the sermon. She left whenever Reverend Rex's preaching started to ramble. She liked to roam the circular hall and look at the soft and whimsical paintings of Jesus, his eyes looking heavenward, and know that he was once a Jew like her. Ellen had never met her Jewish grandparents—some sort of falling out over her parents' marriage—and wasn't quite sure what made a Jew so different from other people. But from overhearing bits of conversation, she was learning: people with curly hair like her own, hard to comb, who couldn't get into Heaven unless they went out to a river and let Rex hold them under the water for a couple seconds.

On Polly and Berta's first Sunday, Ellen had to walk around with them while they were being introduced.

"Not two at a time, Jean! My goodness, how many does that make?"

"Twenty three of the Lord's children have stayed with me over the last ten years. Some stay weeks, some years. Whatever the Lord has planned. A few, you know, have even insisted on changing their last name to Wickle."

"No one is as generous as you and Harold."

"Just my Christian duty."

When they ran into the weasel man's wife, she gave Ellen the once over, and asked Mama Jean if it was true what they said about Jews.

"Oh my, yes, she's my smart one. Smart as a whip!" said Mama Jean, then she looked sadly at Polly, standing slack jawed, in a dress of such cheap fabric that it looked like it could burst into flames if someone aimed a magnifying glass at it too long. "I think she's going to be my dumb one."

On the day of the Bee Keeper, Ellen was too excited to even sit through the singers. She walked round and round the hallway, getting more and more eager. What would the bee keeper do? Call them a special way, in bee language? Tempt them with special bee food? Did he have a musical instrument like the Pied Piper of Hamlin that would charm the bees into following him?

What made it even more exciting was the fact that her mother would like to hear about the event. There wasn't much at the Wickles besides the hens and cocks that she could tell her mother that would not worry her or make her feel bad. But her mother loved nature and educational activities. She had frequently taken Ellen on nature walks at the arboretum and to the Natural History Museum. Ellen remembered a bee exhibit with a slice of honeycomb between two glass panels. Her mother had been fascinated with the frantic bees inside.

On one of her hallway rotations, Ellen noticed Nancy at the bank of pay phones between the restrooms. She leaned against the wall, her lips pressed close to the black mouthpiece. Nancy looked up just as Ellen passed and held a finger to her lips to remind Ellen not to tell. Ellen nodded. There were only two phones in the Wickle house: the kitchen wall phone and the one next to Mama Jean and Harold's bed. None of the foster children were ever, under any circumstances, allowed to enter the Wickles' bedroom. And they were only supposed to use the kitchen phone to talk to their parents (if they had any) or their social worker. Sometimes when Harold and Mama Jean were outside, Nancy sat crouched on the kitchen floor, hidden beneath the windowsill, talking to Hoagie. Her voice always sounded soft and urgent.

❖

The bee keeper pulled into the driveway right after Harold and Mama Jean Wickle. On the side of his green pick-up, "Bee Keeper" and his phone number were hand-painted boldly in white, next to a picture of a bee with a smiling human face. With its goofy face and four wings, the bee looked like a strange angel—just like Berta had said that morning. Two huge wooden boxes rose from the truck bed. When the bee keeper stepped out of the driver's door, the children, who had been filing into the house, stopped in their tracks. The Bee Keeper was dressed in a puffy white space suit, carrying a space helmet under his right arm.

"I left church a little early so I could come up to the house when you did," said the Bee Keeper.

"That was right thoughtful of you, Ralph," said Mama Jean, then she looked at the children. "Stop your gawking, get in the house and change out of them Sunday clothes. Stay inside so none of you don't get stung."

Obediently, they all went in the side door, the boys clattering downstairs while the girls went up to their room. A few minutes later, Ellen was in her slip when Billy shot into the room.

"Have you ever heard of knocking?" asked Nancy. Her arms were crossed over her chest. She wore a frayed white cotton bra, bleached to near brilliance.

With Walter, Ellen thought the failure to knock was lack of proper training. But with Billy, she thought the action was calculated. He affected poor manners in the hope of catching them in an awkward position or—as he just did—a state of undress. This was his fifth foster home. He liked to start fires.

"We're allowed to watch!" shouted Billy. "Outside, up close. The Bee Keeper said it weren't dangerous or nothing. Mama Jean is gonna tell all them people on the road!" The girls dressed much more quickly.

Word had spread fast. By the time Ellen was outside, the event had collected an audience. Everyone sat or stood along the driveway. A few people had mesh-and-aluminum lawn chairs. There was Tin Cole, who still had jet-black hair even though the creases on his face made him look one hundred years old. He lived in a shack down the road. Walter said he used to be an Indian Chief. There was Norma Post. She and her husband spent summers in the nicest trailer on the road while he worked the Northfield Horse Race Track. They spent winters in a place called Hialeah. And there was Mama Jean Wickle's natural son, Jack, and three of his Sheriff department buddies, all wearing dark sunglasses, and their girlfriends, who were going to cook out in Jack's back yard that afternoon.

Ellen sat on the gravel next to Norma Post's lawn chair. Ellen liked to visit her trailer when Mr. Gregg was at the track. When she wasn't lying in the yard on a lounge chair, Norma Post spent her days at the little trailer kitchen booth, playing Solitaire while smoking cigarettes and drinking Cokes. The miniature quality of the room—the table and all the appliances scaled down to fit the tight space—made Ellen feel safe, as if she was in a girl-sized dollhouse.

"I wish Jean Wickle was a card player," said Norma Post, a cigarette dangling from the corner of her mouth, the first time Ellen visited. "It would be nice to have someone to play with."

"Mama Jean Wickle is a Christian," Ellen had said. "They don't play cards."

"I know," said Norma Post, squinting to keep the smoke from her eyes. She was very skinny and tan, with amber-colored hair. She wore a lot of opal rings. "But I could teach you. Jews are good card players."

"Okay," said Ellen. "As long as Mama Jean Wickle doesn't find out."

"She won't," said Norma Post, sweeping up the cards and shuffling the deck. "We know a lot of Jews down at the track in Hialeah." She said it in a friendly way. After that, Ellen went whenever she could get away to play rummy with Norma Post.

❖

The bee keeper stood in the center of the yard between the tree and one of the big wooden boxes, wearing his helmet. A screen-like veil hung in place of where a glass window would be on a real space helmet. He was making a speech about bees. The yard smelled like wet hay, cut grass, and animals. It was hot. Ellen had to fan her face to keep away a persistent fly. She was trying to store every detail of the event in order to tell her mother.

The Bee Keeper said he spoke frequently at schools; he had to speak loudly to be heard through his space helmet and over the buzzing noise. He began with the definition of a bee, "an invertebrate with a segmented body and. . ."

Just at this point, Mama Jean Wickle tapped Ellen on the shoulder.

"Your social worker is on the phone."

"Can she call back?" asked Ellen.

"No, Ellen, honey, this is important, you better go talk to her."

Reluctantly, Ellen rose and dusted off her rear end. A few pieces of gravel were embedded in the part of her behind not covered by her shorts. She trotted into the house. The phone was off the base on the counter. Still wearing his sunglasses, Jack leaned into the refrigerator. His bent form blocked Ellen's path. She had to wait for him to stand before she could pass. He pulled out a six pack of Coke for himself and his friends and closed the refrigerator door. The glass bottles in the cardboard container perspired. Ellen's throat ached. She was very thirsty. The foster children were not allowed to go in the refrigerator on their own. Jack walked past her without saying a word. He never spoke to the foster children. Ellen picked up the phone.

"Hello," said Ellen into the phone.

"Ellen? This is Mrs. Hopper. I have some very sad news for you. Your mother died last night, peaceful in her sleep," Mrs. Hopper took a deep breath. "Ellen? Are you there? Are you okay?"

A large bubble rose in Ellen's dry throat.

"Yes, I'm fine, Mrs. Hopper," said Ellen.

"I will call Mrs. Wickle tomorrow morning about the funeral arrangements," said Mrs. Hopper. "Ellen, I'm very sorry. I wish I could of come out to tell you in person but Sundays are hard for me."

"Yes," said Ellen. "Thank you for calling."

Ellen hung up the phone and went outside. She felt a peculiar dizziness, not faint, just tingly and weightless, as if she were walking in the air, a few inches above the ground. She wove through the people, back to sit cross-legged beside Norma Post's chair. Norma Post put her hand on Ellen's shoulder. Ellen wondered if she knew. Had Mrs. Hopper told Mama Jean Wickle?

The bee keeper was almost finished talking. In Ellen's absence, his speech had taken a dramatic, Christian turn. "They will all follow the Queen Bee, the way we will follow Jesus Christ, our savior, into the gates of heaven."

"Does the queen wear a crown?" asked Polly.

"Shut up, knucklehead," said Walter.

Jack's Adam's apple slid up and down as he drank from his Coke. Ellen thought he was watching her from behind his dark glasses.

She tried to listen to the bee keeper's words, study his movements, but the words and actions blurred together. There was no point now. There was no one to hear the details now.

No one to hear. No one to hear. No one to hear.

Her mother was gone. No longer in the hospital bed. But not in Heaven either. Like Ellen, her mother was a Jew. She had not grown up a Jew but had become one after she married. So her spirit was wandering, fragmented, a hundred winged pieces in the air. In fact, her mother could be among the bees. Ellen fixed her eyes on them, as if with perfect concentration she could see what the others couldn't.

The bee keeper stuck his gloved hand into the churning mass. When he twisted it out, all the bees followed his hand, a wavy

23

thick ribbon of bees. They gathered to form one body, composed of a multitude of dots, floating against the clear blue sky, blindly trailing the queen. A dark road coursing through the air. And for just a moment, while she watched the bees careen toward the wooden box—before the bubble in her throat burst and she began to cry—Ellen felt so light and small that she imagined she had risen to become a part of the winged trail, moving behind the leader who was effortlessly guiding her. And Ellen knew, at that very moment, that, indeed, a part of her mother was in the Queen Bee, every bee, every tree, every blade of grass, and her mother would be inside her too, forever guiding her to a better place.

I have some bad news.

My mother's voice is as distinct as if she is standing next to me. She sounds matter-of-fact, appropriately stricken yet carrying on with a stiff upper lip. Sure of herself. Sure that this news is real, immutable, no one can take that from her—or her from her duty to present it. If I had started counting at a young age, I might have known how many times I had heard these words in this tone issue from my mother's mouth. But there are so many things I could know if I had started counting when I was young. How many kisses? How many men? A few years ago I started keeping lists of books I had read, but I can never reclaim the thousands read before I began this documentation. I mourn the loss of my personal memories even more than I do the list of books—my failures to keep track—as if there is going to be an important court case in some parallel universe for which I will be unprepared. But evidence aside, I have had enough experience to know that my mother's news regards either a bizarre death or a break-up of a couple everyone thought would be together forever. Her favorite tragedies are those brought on by the victims themselves, the result of a character flaw. Oddly, I am certain she takes no pleasure in the news itself, but just as certain that there is pleasure in the telling—a type of satisfaction that is neither malevolent nor indecorous.

What?

I am ashamed of myself for asking, for not pausing longer, for not forcing her to tell me without a prompt. A while ago my mother, lover of delivering bad news, took to refusing to accept any herself—at least from me, without assurance that it wouldn't be the type of bad news she disliked. Instead of asking "what?" she has a series of preliminary screening questions. "How old is the person?" "Have I met her?" "Does it involve cancer?" "Dementia?" If she doesn't like my answers, she might stop me by saying "no, sounds too depressing, I think I'm better off not knowing that." Or worse, if it was someone she knew—an occurrence that has grown less common now that I have lived in Chicago for almost twenty years while she is still in Pennsylvania—she might guess accurately. "I always knew he would leave her" or "she didn't seem well the last time I saw her. She should have exercised." My mother is an expert in bad news, a true connoisseur, practically a psychic, which is strange given her unusually optimistic nature, at least about her own life. And I must say, she has had a lucky life, one in which mostly good things have happened to her.

My mother was a beautiful young woman. I know many people say this about their mothers—particularly writers, actors, and politicians who always seem to have mothers who resembled Rita Hayworth or Marilyn Monroe—thereby ruining the credibility of those of us whose mothers actually were beautiful. Like mine.

My mother married a handsome man, tall and dark with thick curly hair, who was faithful and loving, never had eyes for anyone but her. Neither of them has been seriously ill or suffered any unexpected loss of consequence. Their house was paid off before retirement age and their own parents died peacefully at ripe old ages. If they have one disappointment, it's me, their unmarried, middle-aged daughter. But even that isn't as bad as it might have been. Their son provided them with the requisite grandchildren—a girl and a boy—and I'm not a complete loser. After all, I am a tenured college professor with a reasonable income, nice friends, and my own mortgage. I provide some bragging rights. (She was as good at bragging as she was at presenting distressing news.)

Alice Saunders. It's so sad.

If memory serves me correctly, Alice and her husband were already split up; so Alice had to be dead or dying. The Saunders moved in next door when I was about thirteen. They were younger than my parents—in their mid-twenties—so they didn't socialize much with my parents, though there was an occasional drink before dinner or a neighborhood Christmas party. Because of babysitting for them, I probably saw them more frequently than anyone else in my family. I can't picture her husband's face—though I remember him as athletic and generally good looking, successful, on his way up my parents said—but I have several snapshots of Alice Saunders indelibly sketched in my brain. Alice Saunders in a tangerine colored linen cocktail dress that matched her lipstick. (In the summer she wore bright colors that suited her tan.) Alice Saunders in a bell-shaped maternity smock (before Madonna made tight t-shirts for pregnant women the norm) with a brick-a-brack hem and a gingerbread cookie person between her breasts, a style that seemed incongruous with her otherwise elegant appearance. Alice Saunders lying on a lounge chair in her snow-covered back yard on a sunny day, completely covered except for her face which was trying to catch a tan in the pre-tanning salon days. An aerial view of Alice Saunders traipsing across my lawn as I watched from my upstairs window—the halo of her shiny hair, her bare feet against our green grass—the first time she came over to ask me to babysit. But my strongest image of Alice Saunders is the day they moved in. Trying to stay out of the way of the movers as they carried in the furniture, she sat in the middle of the wide green lawn that sloped up to their house (white, Greek revival style, same as ours). Her tan legs were tucked under her, she wore madras shorts and a plain white linen blouse. Her first born, Ella, I think the name was, was cradled in her lap. Every now and then, Alice lifted the infant above her head to dust her nose against the baby's nose, Eskimo kisses, I heard her call them later. Alice Saunders. She was the type of perfect young mother I wanted to be. Golden hair. Slender tan arms and legs. That was what my parents always called her. Alice Saunders. Not Mrs. Saunders or Alice. Have you heard what happened to Alice Saunders? In the past, what had happened usually concerned her drinking. She had a serious problem. Lots of my parents' friends had drinking problems, some even lost marriages because of drinking. But Alice Saunders' problem was somehow worse: hiding bottles around the house, drinking in closets, forgetting to pick up her children.

I never called Alice Saunders anything. She was too old for me to address as Alice, but too young to be called Mrs. Saunders. When I consider it now, I realize Alice Saunders was probably closer in age to me than to my mother.

Didn't she and her husband split up a long time ago? Her drinking, right? Is she dead?

I have stories in my head of people I barely knew who died in bizarre circumstances. Two young salesmen, members of my parents' post-college crowd, who went down in the crash of a small plane they had chartered for a business trip. Two prostitutes had been aboard with them. (My mother seldom has acquaintances who die quietly in their sleep.) I remember how my mother sighed when she told me, wondering what their young wives, at home with babies in diapers, must have felt at hearing the news of the prostitutes. Had the men lived, their wives would never have known about the prostitutes. But after the news, they would never be able to mourn, never have a chance to forgive. I don't remember those men or their wives, but I carry them around in my memory bank: the crowded plane, laughing young men, faces pink from gin, party girls on their laps, a flash of lightening outside the porthole, screams as the engine sputters and the plane careens, bodies tossing, limbs and bottles flying.

There was the older friend of my mother's who decorated her Christmas tree with miniature furniture—authentic replicas of antiques—from her daughter's dollhouse. The women let me pick a piece the year we visited. I chose a tiny crystal chandelier with dangling prisms the size of rice kernels. I loved it, taped it to the living room ceiling of my tin doll house, until my mother told me the girl and her father had died in a car crash on Christmas Eve. Up until then, I had never wondered where the little girl was or why her mother would decorate a tree with her toys.

29

Some of the stories my mother told me as I was growing up were what one might call "age-appropriate"—or age-inappropriate, depending on one's perspective. In high school, right around the time I had my first spray of adolescent acne, my mother told me about a high school friend of hers who had died from popping a pimple. Apparently, she said, there is an incorrect way of popping a pimple that shoots poison backward through a blood vessel to the brain. It might have been her way of telling me not to meddle with my own blemishes. Quite effective. Not because I was afraid of dying, but because I could not bear the thought of the obituary—"death by pimple popping."

Wait. Let me tell you the whole story. It really is tragic. Ever since she and Arthur divorced, she's always lived out at the Buckingham. He got custody, of course—though the children are long grown now.

Could something worse than death have happened to Alice Saunders? Living in a two-bedroom apartment at the Buckingham complex, with its incongruous mix of mock French provincial detailing, was not as nice as having a house with a wide sloping front lawn, but certainly not a tragedy. After all, it wasn't a studio walk-up out by the railroad tracks. Most of the middle class divorced women in Harmony, Pennsylvania, wound up at the Buckingham—at least until they met their second husbands.

Kathy, my only high school friend of divorced parents, had lived at the Buckingham. I loved visiting her. It seemed extremely sophisticated to be living in an apartment house with a lobby and a doorman, a person to call if something wasn't working properly. All of my other friends lived in houses like me. I had no way of knowing that grown-ups in small towns felt it was better to own their homes than to rent, and didn't enjoy being able to hear what was being said through the walls.

Kathy also lived in Chicago the first year that I was here. She was my only friend in the city at the time. It seemed a unbearably long and unlikely road to tenure, and, worse, Sam had gone back to his wife. He told me the week before Christmas. We had broken up many times before but I knew this time was final. There would not be another breathless evening of making up. My reaction was a disturbing paradoxical mix of panic and grief and relief. To cheer me up, Kathy drove me back and forth on Michigan Avenue to look at the twinkling white fairy lights decorating the trees, while she relayed some her own most humiliating experiences. The one that stands out in my mind was the boy in college who had literally thrown her out of his bed. After being dumped by him, Kathy had gone to his room to try to win him back. He had slept with her but afterward couldn't take her sobbing and begging so had lifted her and carried her, stark naked, into the hallway where he had deposited her before locking his own door. The image of Kathy, alone and naked in the dorm hallway, shocked me out of my own self-pity. I can't remember how she got out of the dilemma; all I retain is an image of her naked—her smooth, young skin— cradled in his arms like a baby, then standing, exposed and unprotected in the hallway. My mother would have enjoyed that story. She disapproved of Kathy because her parents were divorced. It was such a rarity back then that my mother couldn't fathom how a couple couldn't keep their lives patched together. (Now she doesn't understand people who won't leave bad spouses.) I never told her; in addition to being a betrayal of Kathy, I couldn't have borne the concealed satisfaction she would have felt. I preferred to try to tell her stories of tragedies that had befallen women similar to her in age and station in life.

Did it have to do with her drinking?

Not only did the grown-ups whisper about Alice Saunders' drinking. Even I noticed. Whenever I babysat, she was pretty and friendly when they left the house. When they returned, she wasn't able to focus—in fact, it was as if she didn't see me at all —she was capable of nothing but stumbling to the sofa to collapse or to the liquor cabinet where she fixed her myopic gaze on pouring a night cap. Her husband appeared annoyed or distracted as he counted out my pay and asked if I needed to be walked home. I never did; after all, it was western Pennsylvania in the early seventies, which was like other places in the fifties, and I lived right next door.

During my senior, year, I overheard my mother tell my father that Alice Saunders had been sent off to dry out. I pictured an Alice-shaped sponge, saturated, swollen with gin, reclining on a chaise lounge in the sun on the lawn of a huge estate, white-uniformed orderlies and nurses walking the meandering paths around her. The scenario actually seemed romantic to me at the time. I hoped that I might grow into the glamorous type of woman who would need to be sent off to dry out. When I came home from college after my first semester, the Saunders had moved to another, less expensive part of town.

Of course. Drinking was Alice Saunders whole problem. It cost her her husband, her home, her children, and now her life. With some women it's eating, with some it's men. With Alice, it was booze. They found her dead in her apartment.

I knew it—her fate was worse than death—the fact that a "they" had found her meant she was alone. I wondered who the "they" was? Her landlord? A lover? Her former husband and his new wife? Had Mr. Saunders and his new wife continued to watch over her, tuck her in after a binge, then return to their own home on the other side of town? I didn't know for sure that he had a new wife, but I presumed it. A wife to raise his children, a wife who felt sympathy for what he had experienced with Alice, a new wife to comfort him the way I would have comforted Sam if he had left his wife.

Thinking of Sam made me suspicious—what did my mother mean with the remark ". . . with some women it's men?" Was it some sort of subtle rebuke? No, it couldn't be. How could my mother know anything about any of my relationships with men? She lives three states away. And it has been years since I had told her anything of that nature. Still it was troubling; she did seem to have a peculiar psychic ability. When I brought my first boyfriend home in high school, the moment he was out the door she said, "he looks like bad news." It took me almost an entire year to learn the truth of her words. I pushed the thought from my head and tried to imagine how Mr. Saunders had met his second wife.

Perhaps they met at a party while Alice was passed out. Or maybe they met one of the times that Alice was sent away to dry out. Possibly the new wife even made the arrangements for Alice to move into the Buckingham, wrote out the monthly rent checks. I didn't begrudge the new wife. Or Mr. Saunders for leaving Alice—after all he had stuck by her for many difficult years. But, oddly, I was somewhat disappointed in him, the same way I would have been in Sam if he actually had left his wife for me.

I hold my breath, knowing from my mother's tone that there is more to come, the worst part. Most of my mother's stories have little twists at the end, the slightly unbelievable quality of urban legends. Yet I have no doubt they are always true. I might not know the people well, but I know they exist. And I know that my mother never lies. She might have her own version of truth, but she doesn't lie. My mother is such a keen observer of the lives of others that she doesn't need to. She sees things and reports them, but keeps a distance. Sometimes she even states assumptions about the lives of famous people, assumptions that often come true. What is it that draws such an optimistic woman to bad news? A woman whose own life is rich and busy.
Part of her seems to delight in the strange turns life can take, the stories they can make; another part seems to draw reassurance from the fact that the cause is actually right there, embedded in the life. Are the stories meant to be collected and parceled out as lessons to those who are less capable and controlled than she?

Who found her?

It is interesting how much of any conversation takes place in the minds of the participants. That is one of the reasons why, I think, shared memories seldom match—the bulk of conversations take place where only one of the parties has access. This is why Sam would tell the story of our affair differently than I. Why my mother's version of my childhood and my own would probably differ vastly.

That's the worst part. Ella and her youngest son, Alice Saunders' grandson. You remember Ella, don't you? She was the oldest. She had brought her son to visit his grandmother and there she was—dead!

I remembered Ella in diapers, seersucker play suits, startled by her own ability to walk across her parents' living room, looking at each foot as it came up as if it were a miracle. And of course, that day on the front lawn when the Saunders moved in, dusting noses with her mother, Alice. A quick calculation told me that she must be in her late thirties now. Almost a generation older than my students. At forty-eight, I had just reached the age where I could tell students stories from my youth that shocked them because they sounded so old fashioned. Stories of wearing white gloves on airplanes and for trips into the city, typing essays with carbon papers, cigarettes for 55 cents a pack. Life for them would have been unbearable without DVD's, only three channels, and no call-waiting or cell phones. Whenever I tell these things, I see the astonishment on their faces, as if they are trying to reconcile what I say with how I look—not much older than their parents, perhaps even younger in terms of style and dress, a result of spending so much time on campus. Or maybe their astonishment has to do with something else? That I would tell them these things at all? That I think these items from my past interesting or pertinent to their lives?

I am growing annoyed.

Just tell me. What happened?

A friend of my father's who had squandered his family's fortune, had, before killing himself, gone out to the golf course, spread an oil cloth by the 18th hole—as not to soil the green—then shot himself in the head. At the time, my mother had remarked that at least he had been considerate enough to do it in a place where his wife wouldn't find his body. The obituary had simply read he died at Green Valley Golf Club. Those who didn't know would assume a heart attack. What would my students think of that?

I think my mother detects the irritation in my tone. She speeds up her tale.

Apparently she had just been released from a detox center— not a very nice one, I gather—and they told her this was it, she would really need to quit this time or that was it, she would die. She had just gotten out that day, stopped at the grocery store on her way home, one bag on the kitchen counter next to an open

bottle of wine. There was a glass in her hand. The other grocery
bags were still in the car.

I wonder, is this possible? If a doctor tells you that you'll die if you continue drinking, can one simple glass of wine literally finish you off? Or had my mother omitted a few crucial details?

I picture the stem of the glass between Alice's fingers, her head thrown back against the sofa, while outside two brown paper bags sit in the open hatchback of a Honda. Why a Honda — because that's what I drive? That's ridiculous! I have nothing in common with Alice. I rarely even finish a glass of wine. Yet when I roll the images around in my head, I think I understand how she must have felt, not being able to wait until she had even brought in all the bags. The sound of the cork being plucked from the bottle; the sparkle of white wine being poured into a goblet; the overwhelming rush of the first sip; and, most important, the feelings it must have evoked—anticipation, guilt, longing, relief. Although I don't have a big taste for alcohol, I know the feeling of desire, of drowning in your own cure for pain. Haven't I felt that at the smell of a lover's skin, the taste of Sam's sweat?

How do you know all of this?

I often forget to ask this question. And I never ask why she has chosen to tell me, what she wants me to take from the story. I know that I am supposed to figure that out on my own. That much I know about our relationship. We are seldom able to say what we mean directly. Do all families invent their own forms of saying what they want to say, buried in stories and gossip and news? Their own method of delivery, nudging questions from the listener, forcing silences in order to increase or decrease the other's culpability in the telling of bad news? Or could it be that I've misjudged my mother? Might she have entirely different intentions than the ones I perceive? Could her bad news be intended as good? Might she be saying that things could be worse?

Look, I would love to chat, but the Parkers are coming for dinner tonight and I haven't even gone to the store yet. Your father is going to be home any minute.

Then she is gone. I am left holding a dead line. This is just another of my mother's peculiarities—ending conversations and hanging up, without saying goodbye—for which, despite all the hundreds of times it has happened, I am still unprepared.

THE WOMAN WITH THE LONGEST HAIR

After much inner turmoil and struggle, Susie decided to cut her hair. It might have been the most momentous decision in her life—certainly one of the most anxiety-provoking ones. She had been postponing the event ever since she was five years old, and had refused to let her mother trim her hair. In fact, she had run away, hid out overnight in a huge drainage pipe just to avoid the snap of the scissors. When she walked home at sunrise, her socks and sneakers were so wet that her toes were pruned to little raisins. She actually lost one nail that never grew back correctly.

Three police cruisers were waiting in her parents' driveway. Some neighbors had brought food. And her grandparents had flown all the way up from Florida. Her mother hugged her so hard that Susie felt as if she were made of Play Doh. Of course, her mother promised never to come near her with scissors again.

After that, Susie's hair was her crown. She could do whatever she desired with it. Her father, usually a taciturn man, who spent most evenings in his chair with the paper, said she was spoiled because she was the youngest. But Susie knew it was because her mother had made a pact with God. Send my daughter back alive and I will worship her hair. Her mother bought her every hair ribbon, barrette, and headband she wanted. Susie wore pig tails, braids, buns, even a French twist while still in the fourth grade. Though most often she wore a pony tail. In sixth grade, when the girls liked to play horse at recess, she was the envy of the others. She could whinny and snort and dig her hoofs better than anyone. It was almost as if the twitch of her long ponytail imbued her with a special horse spirit.

She frequently got the best parts in the school plays—the princess, the angel, the fairy queen, and, naturally, Rapunzel. Short haired girls got witch parts or, worse, had to play boys.

But as her long hair continued to grow—past her shoulders, down her back, below her waist—it ceased being an emblem of strength and independence, and became a weight. It wasn't anything Susie could put her finger on—or was even aware of at all times—just a general uneasiness that prevented her from fully enjoying her hair's magnificence. By the time she was thirty, her beautiful rippling locks swung beneath her knees; her devotion to her hair was equaled only by her apprehension about it. She felt driven to test herself, as well as her husband, Alan.

When she told Helen, her hairdresser, owner of the Curl Up and Dye Beauty Parlor, she wanted a cut, Helen misunderstood. She though Susie meant a trim.

"No," said Susie firmly, sitting straight up in the beautician's swivel chair, her long hair covering her shoulders like a dramatic cape. "All at once, right below my ears."

"But don't you want to have a chance to get used to it, decide over time, gradually, if you truly want to go that short?" asked Helen, worried, her eyebrows shooting up like a tiny draw bridge opening to make way for a ship. That was one of the things Susie liked about Helen, why she had been coming here so long. Helen was older and dumpier than other beauticians Susie had tried, but she was responsible. The first time Susie visited her, Helen simply followed her instructions. Most hairdressers, at initial appointments, took a fistful of Susie's hair, and said, "Why don't you let me get rid of this for you," as if her hair was an annoying pest. While Susie wondered if they were right, she suspected them of jealousy.

"If I get it cut gradually, I won't be able to save it all in one piece," said Susie.

"You have a point," said Helen. "Do you want me to do it now? I wish you had told me before I washed it."

"No, next week. I want to make a special appointment. It will be the most important day of my life, so I want to arrange everything I do next week around it," said Susie. "Oh, and I will want a wash first—a double wash; I want what I save to be sparkling clean."

❖

That night when Susie and Alan were watching television, Helen called to ask Susie's permission to contact a reporter at the local paper to write a story about the event. Helen said that she wanted the moment documented so Susie could show her children and grandchildren. Susie suspected Helen actually wanted the publicity, was envisioning headlines: WORLD'S BEST HAIRDRESSER ENTRUSTED TO CUT LONGEST LOCKS. But Susie didn't care. She rather liked the idea of a newspaper article. When she hung up and sat back down next to Alan on the couch, in the glow of the television screen, she told him there might be a story in the paper. Alan took a handful of her hair, a river running through his palm, lifted it to his lips, and kissed it. "I'm going to miss your hair," he said. "I wish you would reconsider." She tugged her hair away, a little guiltily. Though it seemed too ridiculous to say aloud, Alan was the reason she had first thought of cutting it. The last few times he had helped her wash it, a voice inside her head had whispered *not his, not his.* She loved her hair, knew it was beautiful, but the voice—in connection with Alan's adoration— contributed to her growing anxiety. She had to test them both.

To assuage her guilt, Susie kissed Alan lightly on the cheek. *Not his, not his.*

"I know," she said. "I love my hair even more than you do." She thought she would tell him about the whisper years from now, once they had discovered all the things that were special between them besides her hair, and they would laugh.

❖

As she sat, again, in the swivel chair, all dressed up, her hair twice washed, waiting for the reporter, the promise of the article was all that kept Susie from fleeing the beauty parlor. Her fear of the whisper seemed silly. Shouldn't she be happy that Alan loved her hair as much as he did?

Susie twisted one long cord around and around her right thumb. Around and around and around. Helen had canceled all her afternoon appointments to concentrate on Susie and the reporter. Susie couldn't just bolt.

When the reporter sauntered in, nearly twenty minutes late, Susie disliked her on sight. Leah wore tight black jeans and a shrunken black top revealing a pierced belly button. Her hair was clipped short, brushed away from her face, dyed so that it had a purplish hue. Her finger nails were the same color. Her nostrils were flared in a way that revealed the pinkish-yellow inner membrane. Susie had seen women who dressed like Leah in magazines and on MTV, but rarely in Park Town—or any other part of Butler County for that matter. Susie had delivered a classified ad to the newspaper office once; the place was situated in an old house. Two desks sat in what used to be the living room and two in the former dining room. Susie doubted they had more than two or three reporters.

"Hi, you must be Susie," Leah said, thrusting her right hand in Susie's lap to shake. "I could tell by your hair."

Helen laughed, more heartily than the joke required.

In her left hand, Leah carried a stenographer's pad. A professional looking black camera was slung over her shoulder. Leah's smile was so bright, her grip so firm, that Susie's initial distaste vanished.

Susie smiled. She felt shy.

"Do you live in Park Town?" she managed to ask, wanting to appear polite, not so self-centered as a person in her situation might seem.

"No, I drive up from Pittsburgh a couple days a week. I'm still in school; when I graduate I'll probably head for New York or L.A.," Leah said as she made adjustments on her camera, snapping parts open and closed, peering inside. "I'm going to be an investigative reporter."

"Oh, my husband goes down to Pittsburgh to work a lot," said Susie, immediately embarrassed. She didn't want to look like she was bragging that she was married. Leah wore no ring.

First, Leah snapped a lot of photographs. From the front, the back, the side. She took one of Susie standing on a chair. One of Helen half way across the room, holding Susie's hair out like a road block. Another of Helen brushing Susie's hair. Leah even crouched down on the floor to take a shot looking up at Susie. All the attention dissolved Susie's shyness. She felt adventurous to be cutting her hair, spontaneous, maybe even brave to be willing to give up something so beautiful.

Next, while Helen braided Susie's hair in preparation for the cut, Leah conducted the interview. She had an earnest way of asking questions that made Susie recall things she had long forgotten. She told how she usually got to play the princess in school plays. How well she could pretend to be a horse. She told about some of the different ways she wore her hair. All the ribbons and bows she owned as a girl. She even revealed how she had hidden in the drainage pipe.

"Surely it must also be inconvenient?" asked Leah. She had exquisite blue eyes, as pale and translucent as marbles.

Susie shrugged. Until the voice, the strange whisper, she had always thought she loved her hair.

"I mean there must be problems with having hair so long," prompted Leah. "I bet it can even be dangerous."

"Well, I do have to be careful around electric fans." Leah wrote that down.

"And when my husband and I went to the courthouse, back in Ohio, to apply for our marriage license, it got caught in the elevator door. Fortunately, Alan is quick on his feet. He pushed the OPEN DOOR button just in the nick of time." Leah wrote that down.

"How does your husband like your hair?"

"He loves it."

"Was it what attracted him to you in the first place?"

44

"He said it was the first thing he noticed about me."

"I bet," snorted Leah, and wrote again in her steno pad. "Do you have to spend a lot of time taking care of it? Is it difficult to keep clean?"

"Well, I generally spend about an hour on it a day, sometimes up to two, brushing or fixing it. Usually, my husband, Alan, helps me wash it," said Susie. "But I come to Helen twice a month to give us a break."

"I have many fine products for girls with long hair," said Helen. Past the midway point on the braid, Helen was now about a foot and a half from Susie's chair. The braid hung between them like a rope bridge. "Long hair is one of my specialties. So are dyes, frostings, and perms. Twice a week, I have a girl in to do nails. My rates are the lowest in the area."

"Uh-huh," said Leah. She didn't write any of what Helen said. "So, Susie, what made you decide to get it cut now?"

"I'm not sure," she said, thinking the story of the whisper would make her sound wacky in the article. "It was my thirtieth birthday last week, and I wanted a change. With summer coming up, it seemed like a good time. My hair can get pretty hot."

Helen finished braiding, and wound the thin tip in a rubber band.

"Well, here goes," said Helen, lifting the huge pair of silver shears from the counter. She paused. "You ready, Susie?" Susie took a deep breath.

"Uh-huh," she said.

Helen wrapped the braid around her hand and held it tautly. The metal felt cold against the nape of Susie's neck. The cut made a crunching sound. After three bites, the scissors blades clicked together in one final lop. Leah snapped a picture. Helen handed Susie her braid. She held it above her head, away from her body, like a prize fish. Leah took another photograph. The entire cut had taken less than a minute. The hair she had spent twenty-five years growing was now gone.

"How do you feel?" asked Leah.

"Good," said Susie, trying to swallow. Her mouth felt dry. Leah asked a few more questions about Susie's marriage, her family, her education, and her occupation. Then she slapped her notebook shut and shook hands with both Susie and Helen.

"Thanks a lot," said Leah, slinging her camera over her shoulder.

"When will the story be in the paper?" asked Helen.

"Can't really say," said Leah, her hand on the doorknob. "Probably the middle of next week. Since it's not hard news, they'll wait for a light day."

"Thank you," said Helen.

"Yes, thank you very much," said Susie.

As soon as the door swung shut behind Leah, Susie picked up a hand mirror. She had a hard time looking at her hair. Instead she concentrated on her eyes, as if they would tell her how the haircut had changed her.

"Next week, when it's grown out a little, you can come back and I'll shape it for free," said Helen. While she talked, Helen raked her fingers upwards through Susie's hair, an attempt to fluff it out around her ears, make it appear fuller.

Susie waited impatiently for Alan to get home from work, returning to the bathroom every few minutes to look at her hair in the medicine cabinet mirror. She tilted her head this way and that. Did her eyes look bigger? Her face broader? She tried to convince herself that she had done the right thing, but with each passing moment, her spirits sank lower and lower. Her face looked plain without her hair, clear skin, nice features— two eyes, a nose, a mouth—yet nothing remarkable.

When Alan walked in the door and looked at her, Susie howled. His expression was an unmistakable mix of loss and disappointment. Susie ran into the bathroom and locked the door. Staring at her reflection, she sobbed and sobbed. The wash of tears turned her eyes an emerald green.

"Come on, baby, it looks fine. Really it does. Please open the door," Alan pleaded from the other side. "Please."

She didn't come out until it was too late to make dinner and they had to go to McDonald's. They ate their hamburgers in the car on the way home because Susie didn't want Alan looking at her while she ate. The beef tasted like sand in her mouth.

❖

That night, after they made love, Susie lay on her back, staring at the ceiling, remembering her wedding day. Over a hundred live flowers were woven into her hair. The "ohhh's" and "ahhh's" from the crowd as she walked up the aisle were overwhelming.

At the reception she tried not to turn her head much so she wouldn't lose any of the flora. She didn't even lean back to sip her champagne or to let Alan feed her cake. She had left the flowers in for her wedding night. When she had walked out of the hotel bathroom, naked except for the flowers, Alan had said, "You look just like Eve. Alan and Eve."

In the morning, the sheets were stained with green stems and strewn with flower petals.

❁

Each day, Susie felt worse. For nearly a week, she called in sick to her job at J.C. Penny's. The funny thing was, she really did feel sick. Her head felt so light that she kept imagining that it was going to float up and off her neck, ascending into the blue skies like a helium balloon. She walked around with her hand on top of her skull as if holding it in place. Then she imagined her head was shrinking. Next she imagined it was growing. She recalled a girl she had known in kindergarten with water on the brain. The girls' head was so big that she didn't have the strength to carry it on her own, so she had to be pushed around in a wheel chair.

Only Susie's hopes regarding the newspaper article kept her going. Whenever she felt herself slipping too low, she imagined herself buying twenty copies of the issue with her story, neatly clipping the article from each paper, and mailing it to relatives.

By most standards, Susie was less successful than her six older brothers and sisters. Except for Karen, Susie was the only one who didn't attend college. And Karen had appeared in two made-for-television movies. Her other sisters had married wealthy men. And her oldest brother, Peter, was a dentist. All Susie had was her hair. She wouldn't have even left Ohio if she hadn't met Alan. She was working at a J.C. Penny near Akron when he visited her store as part of an independent auditing team. He was an accountant, but he said looking at Susie made him feel like a poet. She felt important when he asked her to move to Park Town in Pennsylvania, an hour north of Pittsburgh. Now that her hair was gone, the newspaper article describing her act of courage was all she had to show she was special.

She bought a package of expensive museum cards, planning to send one to each of her brothers and sisters, once she had the article. Inside them, she would write, "Enclosed is a little article the paper wrote up about me. I thought you would get a kick out of it."

First thing each morning, she would dart out of their little duplex, still in her pajamas, to retrieve the paper. She would scour each page. If the paper didn't arrive until she was in the shower, she would burst from the bathroom the moment she heard Alan open the front door. Alan would greet her expectant face with the words, "Not today." Three weeks after the interview, Susie was washing her hair, thinking of calling Leah, planning her wording, when Alan knocked on the bathroom door.

"Pay dirt," he said.

Nearly slipping, Susie jumped over the rim of the tub and grabbed a towel. She didn't even rinse the soap out of her hair.

"Give me that paper," she said to Alan as she snatched it from his hands. "I want to read it first."

"All right already," Alan said. Their relationship hadn't been going so well since the haircut. They hadn't made love in weeks. Her hair had always been an important part of their sex life. Sometimes she would pinch a bunch of her ends together, like a paint brush, and run it up and down Alan's torso to excite him. He would wrap his hands in the thick mass to pull her body to his. Sometimes, riding him, she draped her hair over him, making a private tent. Other times she swung it around like wings. And when he entered her from behind, he held onto bands of hair as if they were reins.

Now they were just two ordinary people who rarely talked to each other. But was that really a change? As hard as she tried, she couldn't remember a single conversation they had before the hair cut that wasn't either part of the business of living together or what now seemed silly romantic ramblings. Sentimental tributes from Alan. She hoped their relationship was deeper than her memory of it.

Spreading the paper out on the kitchen table, Susie tucked a corner of the towel between her breasts to secure it. Her hair dripped on the paper, spotting the pages with gray water marks. Her wet fingers dissolved the edges as she turned. What did it matter? She would be buying plenty more.

The article covered the entire top of the fourth page in the features section. They had used three photographs: the one Leah had taken from the floor, looking up at Susie (not a very flattering angle—Susie appeared to have a double chin); one of Helen holding the braid poised between the scissors blades; and the one of Susie holding up the braid like a caught fish. She smiled only in the last one, and it was a tentative smile, at best. Susie began to read.

By Leah Wilham

If you think the days of the un-informed woman, willing to suffer the discomforts of tight girdles and hours of preparation just to please a man, are over—think again. Apparently not every woman in Butler County has heard the word, feminism.

Susie Cook, 30, went for twenty-five years without a haircut because she believed her unusually long hair made her "pretty." She said her hair helped her attract boys and get parts as the princess and the angel in school plays.

"It was the first thing my husband noticed about me," said Cook.

Despite the fact that it takes two people to wash her hair and the long strands frequently get caught in electric fans and elevator doors, Cook has clung to the one thing that she believes makes her special. Instead of attending college, Cook took a part-time job at J.C. Penny's so she would have the two hours she needs each day to maintain her hairstyle . . .

Susie was barely able to comprehend the next dozen or so paragraphs, her mind was in such a jumble. A lot was about post-feminism and women forgetting the Women's Liberation Movement. Japanese women who bound their feet. Dehumanization. Playboy bunnies. The last line read, "Perhaps now, without the burden of her hair, Cook will have the opportunity to learn what it really means to be a woman—that is, a woman who relies more on her brains, than her looks, to get ahead in life."

Susie tried to rise from her chair. She couldn't stand straight. Slanting forward, she had difficulty walking. Her legs felt leaden. Holding on to furniture for support, she made it to the bedroom where she climbed under the sheets. Alan followed her. As she placed her head on her pillow, she could hear the fizzle of the soap bubbles dissolving in her hair.

"What is it honey? What's the matter? Are you sick?"

"The article," she managed to croak before turning her face into the pillow. Alan returned to the kitchen to read it. A few minutes later, Susie heard the front door slam.

❖

Susie quit her job at J.C. Penny.

Alan had little to say about her resignation.

"You know, we're not going to be able to eat out much without your salary." Susie didn't reply. How could she? Did he think that all her hair meant was a trip now and then to the Red Lobster? The evening of the article, he had come home from work and apologized for leaving so abruptly. He said the right things—what he should have said that morning: that Susie was beautiful with or without her hair. He ranted that the reporter was unprofessional, jealous, crazy, carrying on like she was some big city political writer, not just a small town features writer. He even offered to call up the editor at the paper and complain, but Susie declined. It was too late.

Their relationship was forever changed.

Susie never went back to the Curl Up and Dye for that free shaping Helen had offered. In fact, Susie rarely ventured out at all. She spent most of June and July lying in their postage stamp-sized backyard, on a huge beach towel, reading. Once a week, she went to the library, picked up three new books, and returned the three from the previous week. Since the librarian hadn't known Susie when she had long hair, she was one of the few people Susie could stand seeing face-to-face. During one visit, the librarian had said, "You look familiar. Don't I know you from somewhere? Were you ever in the newspaper?"

"My sister looks a lot like me. She's on television sometimes," said Susie. "I'm nobody."

At first, Susie's acquisitions were based on the librarian's recommendations. But the more Susie read, the more the words seemed to trigger questions, ideas—even interests—that would help her with her next week's selections. She could hardly read fast enough to get to the next thing she wanted to know, to feel.

❖

Toward the end of the summer, Alan came home from work early one day and walked out to the backyard to stand over her on the towel. Twisting to look up at him, Susie used her hand to shield her eyes from the sun.

"I'm leaving," said Alan. "I want a divorce."

"Don't let the door hit you on the way out," said Susie and turned back to her book. She had reached an exciting part of *Sense and Sensibility*, a scene that seemed much more real than the one in her backyard with Alan.

Considering this last remark, Alan was very generous. He let Susie keep their modest savings and agreed to pay both her utilities and rent until their lease ran out at the end of September. He even volunteered to pay for Susie's move back to her parents' house in Ohio. She sent away for an application to the University of Akron, and was accepted for winter semester. She spent hours going over the catalog, trying to decide what courses she would take. She changed her library acquisitions from novels to nonfiction books on subjects she thought she might like to study: sociology, art history, and archeology.

It took Susie most of September to pack. She would read a chapter of a book, load part of a box, then read another chapter. Every box took several hours. Particularly since she liked to carefully examine each item before she packed it.

She was cleaning out a junk drawer in the utility room when she came across it, under a mess of large brown envelopes, tangled rubber bands and string, broken pencils, and old accounting ledgers: her braid, coiled like a strange bird's nest in the bottom of the drawer.

Gently, with both hands, she lifted the mound from the drawer. She had given it to Alan as a gift the night of the haircut, after they had gone to McDonald's, a make-up present, before bed. She cradled the mass lovingly in her fingers, held it to her face, inhaled the fragrance of shampoo, reminiscent of the many hours she had spent at Helen's, and the deep smell of her childhood: the playground, the school plays, even the dank drainage pipe where she had sat for so many dark hours. Then she slid the hair garland into one of the brown envelopes, sealed it, and addressed the fat package to Leah Wilham at the newspaper office. Susie returned to the couch, picked up her book, and tried to read, but she couldn't stop her mind from racing, daydreaming about all the things she would do once she was back home, now that she was finally free. She wondered if Leah could ever guess that her one small act of meanness had had such an impact on Susie's life? She considered reopening the package to Leah, adding a thank-you note, but finally decided to let her hair speak for her—one last time.

While rinsing her lunch dish and glass, Corrine looked out the window at the man hired to erect the fence. The man was tall and lanky with a scruffy beard and dirty jeans. Though homeless or near homeless, he might—with a sports jacket— have looked like a professor in her department. He had an intelligent face. At least his intense eyes, along with his high forehead and the deep furrow between his brows, suggested intelligence. She realized that the crevice could just as easily have been caused by trying to understand matters beyond his grasp, and that intense-looking eyes were sometimes the result of drugs or madness.

Corrine placed the round blue dish in the strainer, and leaned across the sink on her forearms to watch him. He had been there since she got up, yet had only managed to sink one post. He was standing back to study it, tilting his head, the way an artist might to contemplate a painting. Corrine had planned to ride her bike out Old County Line Road to the nursery after lunch. Although she could only carry back a few cuttings in her basket, she could get an idea of what she wanted for the far back section, by the new fence, before she and Hank, her husband, returned with the car for larger plants. Hank had promised to take her as soon as he submitted the paper he was writing, his latest analysis of Gallipoli. At least another three days. Perhaps she should wait until then to buy the cuttings? She dreaded passing the man in the yard to get her bike from the garage. Her hesitation wasn't fear or snobbery. It just felt rude, intruding on him that way, catching him paused in the intimacy of assessing his work, as if she was silently criticizing his lack of progress.

She needed a way to soften the discomfort of walking by him. She wasn't the type to have a pitcher of homemade lemonade, but there were a couple of cans of Diet Coke in the fridge. She grabbed one and headed for the yard. The man looked over at the sound of the screen door banging.

"Hi, I'm Corrine Culbertson," she said, passing him the icy can. "I thought you could use a cold drink."

He nodded gravely, accepting the can with a long outstretched arm. She noticed the black arches of dirt beneath his fingernails. Suddenly, Corrine felt embarrassed, almost ashamed. Why hadn't she brought a glass with ice?

"Well, good luck today," said Corrine, more chipper than intended. "I'm going for a bike ride." Again, he nodded.

❖

The fence came in sheets of six connected vertical planks. The only real work was sinking the posts and attaching the sheets, tasks that should have taken about the same time the man had spent installing the single post. For a nominal fee, a person from Home and Garden Supply would have done the whole job in a single afternoon. That had been the original plan. Then Hank had met the ponderous man at the concrete chess tables in the town square.

"He has a rating of twenty-one fifty? Can you believe it?" Hank had asked.

"What does that have to do with installing a fence?" Corrine had countered.

"He's been out of work for a long time."

"Oh," said Corrine. Oh, such a short and quiet word of exclamation, yet so loaded with meaning. It was because of Winston. Hank had hired the man because of Winston. Wherever Winston was at that moment, he was probably out of work too.

❖

In their small Ohio town, the college where they both taught supplied the main source of employment. Except for the campus, the town was shabby: two dozen shops pulled up to the town square like needy relatives gathered at table for a free meal. Two used bookstores. A dress store. A hardware store. A second-run movie house. An ice cream shop. Corrine and Hank often wondered how the places stayed in business.

The town collected drifters. In the seventies when Corrine started in the English Department, the poor had blended in with the fading hippie population of students and young professors. Now they stood out. Once, when coming out of the ice cream shop, licking a scoop of raspberry swirl in a sugar cone, Corrine had seen three police officers attempting to remove a dead man from the backseat of a car. A vagrant who had discovered an unlocked door, he had fallen asleep in the car and died. He was difficult to extricate because rigor-mortis had set in, freezing him in a slouching position. Though Corrine had only had a few licks of her cone, she tossed it in the trash. The taste stayed on her tongue all day.

It felt good, after a winter of walking carefully on slippery streets, and then a muddy spring, to be on her bike again, her legs forcing the pedals around. At the southern corner of Forest and Oak, Corrine passed a bed of daffodils, fifty or more frilly bursts of yellow. She felt a lightness that she hadn't experienced in a long time.

For years, their house had been chaotic with laundry, children, grading papers, and planning lectures. She didn't know much about gardening and hadn't had time to learn. Besides, the earth immediately around the house was too shadowy for much besides ferns, which she had planted in a half-hearted way over the years since Winston left. But now she was ready for a large sunny garden at the far back of the yard, the one place where the light hit at eleven in the morning and didn't recede until late afternoon, the spot where Winston used to play. Once when Winston was little, he had spent an entire day, from morning to dark, building a complex highway there for his Matchbox cars, an intricate system with Popsicle stick overpasses. She and Hank had speculated that he would become an engineer. When Winston hit his teen years, the Phisters, who lived behind them, purchased a big slobbering dog that liked to dig and sleep in the sunny spot. Last winter the dog died.

Corrine was anxious to get the fence up before the Phisters got a new dog, making such a gesture appear un-neighborly. With a fence, she could have a real garden to nurture in privacy. In January, she had spent her spare time reading about gardens. Then, at the first indication that winter was over, they had tilled a large bed and bought supplies for the fence. She wanted color. She wanted to learn how to grow perennials, plants that returned each year stronger and more rooted than the year before.

She and Hank had lived in the same house since they married, which was shortly after she was hired by the college. At the time, Hank was already a full professor in the History Department. She was an Assistant Professor in the English Department; her area of research was folk and fairy tales. She remembered how Hank had laughed when she had told him.

"So, what will the college think of next? Now, they're hiring experts in things that never happened," he said.

"Like your version of history did happen," she had retorted.

Again, he laughed, and said, "Touché."

Despite her feisty reply, she had secretly agreed with Hank. He seemed like a real professor, one who had done all the right things, gone to a good college immediately after high school, then on to earn his doctorate, and study serious matters of war. Corrine felt like someone who had just landed in academia through a series of lucky coincidences. She had married young, had had two children, David and Ruth, and had been divorced before she finished college or started grad school. It was just luck that she developed a clever thesis on fairy tales and feminism at just the time when such things were trendy and publishable.

Two years after she married Hank, who had been too dedicated to his work for a first marriage, she gave birth to Winston.

At the nursery, Corrine was surprised to find her eyes drawn more to the shade section than the sunny one. Perhaps it was because the day was so cloudless and bright. The oranges and pinks seemed gaudy. How, she wondered, could a flower, an act of nature, be gaudy? Nature couldn't have poor taste, could it? Though she remembered that her mother had never ordered flowers for an event or a new baby without saying "Absolutely no carnations. Too tacky."

On the bike ride home, her basket contained only a few small astilbes, shade plants that would bloom a subtle white. She thought that while she waited for the fence to be finished, she could plant the hints of color on either side of their shady front door. When she rounded into her driveway, the man was gone, the posts and sheets in two neat stacks, his empty Coke can on the back porch. He had not completed anything beyond the first post. She hoped they wouldn't have to fire him.

❖

Around two a.m., the phone rang, waking her from a deep sleep. Though she felt a slight stab in her chest at being woken by the loud trill next to her head, she had learned, over the years, to subdue her immediate fear. Without rising, she dragged the receiver to her ear. Hank lifted himself up to lean on his right elbow, a position that would allow him to move into action if needed.

"Hi Mom, it's me," said Winston. His voice a little slurred. Drunk? On drugs? At least he was alive. "Hello, Winston."

Hank sank back down.

The first time Winston called late at night was a week after he had taken off, right before his eighteenth birthday. She had screamed at him, for leaving, for not calling sooner, and, then, when he did call, for doing so in the middle of night, scaring her out of her wits. He had hung up on her and not called back for six months. They had hired a detective, contacted various shelters around the country, and put personal ads in newspapers in all the major cities. The entire time, she had felt a blood bubble rising in her throat, swelling, on the verge of popping, each time the phone rang. By the time he did call again, she had learned to hide her emotions, act calmly, as if a chatty phone call from one's disappeared son in the middle of the night was a normal occurrence. That was almost eight years ago.

"Where are you, Winston?" Though he never answered this question specifically, it usually didn't hurt to ask.

"In the mountains, Mom. You would not believe this view! Oh, my God, we've been hiking all day. We just came back to camp. I gave this dude five bucks to use his cell phone; he's got all these free minutes. Know what I mean? I didn't think it'd work up here. You should have seen this ledge we were on, a sheer drop, must have been seven thousand feet. At sunset, the sky was like those strawberries and cream things granny used to make."

Her heart ached. Unlike her other children, Winston was passionate about everything, interested in pursuing nothing. She remembered how after spending nine hours furiously constructing the maze of highways in the dirt, he just abandoned the whole project, left the Matchbox cars out to rust in the rain and sun. She didn't understand. Her older children had always taken good care of their belongings.

"Who is the 'we'?"

"Ah, mom, it doesn't matter," he said, his words a slurred sigh. "You don't known none of them."

There was no point in correcting his grammar. Just as there had been no point in asking who he was with, but over the years since he had vanished, she had grown so accustomed to trying to pry clues that she did it unconsciously.

"I'm just curious."

"Can't you just listen to what I'm saying, what I'm telling you? Why are you only curious about what isn't there?"

"I'm sorry—tell me about the mountains—or about whatever you want to tell me."

She listened to his rambling, punctuated with the short puffs of cigarette smoke, aware of Hank frozen beside her, his whole being tense, straining not to hope he would be called to the phone, until Winston ended with, "Hey, this dude wants his phone back."

❖

The fence builder had a second post planted before she was out of bed, and a third set before she left for the college to turn in her grades. Corrine felt an odd sense of pride—and relief. He was going to do it, he was going to get the fence up; they wouldn't have to go through the pain and embarrassment of dismissing him. Hank wasn't going to have to experience a new sense of loss.

The fence builder's progress gave her energy to help get her through the day after Winston's call. She only felt half awake. She always had difficulty returning to sleep after a phone call from Winston. First, there were the five or ten minutes she needed to repeat to Hank what had been said. Next, there were the twenty or thirty minutes they spent re-assuring each other that Winston was probably fine, that at least he had friends—he had said hiking with friends—that he had the wherewithal to call them, that he was still in his twenties, still had time to return to a normal life. Then, came the worst part, lying awake all night, no longer talking, simply staring at the darkness, wondering where they had gone wrong.

As a baby, he was different from Ruth and David. More lively, more curious, more easily excited, more easily hurt. Corrine had attributed these differences to a brilliance her other children hadn't had. Their father had been nothing more than average. A good-looking boy whom she had run away with the week she graduated from high school. She saw Winston's father as exceptional. At the top of his class in both high school and college, he had pursued history with passion and patience. Hank was pure, a man who tried to understand what happened in the past without any ulterior motives. And weren't sons supposed to surpass their fathers?

David and Ruth had surpassed their father. They were well behaved, and they had excelled in school. They were good and she loved them. But Corrine had had neither the experience nor the resources to provide for them the way she could for Winston. She had been a young mother, working and going to school during their childhoods. Even their names seemed commonplace when compared to Winston's. She had named David after his father without a second thought. In fact, she hadn't even discussed it with him beforehand. She just filled out the hospital forms based on a tacit assumption. Ruth was named after Corrine's mother. Yet, she and Hank had spent months deciding on Winston's name. She had taken off a semester after his birth, followed by a summer, then by a reduced course load until he was three years old, and Hank arranged his schedule so that he was there when she wasn't. Winston was the only child of the three to whom she could devote real attention. The only one raised in a two-parent home from birth. She thought it was going to be wonderful to have a chance—and the time—to raise a child properly.

Only, it hadn't gone as expected. David and Ruth's teachers had had only praise for them. With Winston, there was always a "He's very bright, tests well . . . but," followed by a list of things he hadn't done or bad things he had. Like most mothers—all mothers in fairy tales—the worse he was, the more she loved him.

In junior high, the real problems started. Hank couldn't accept Winston's inability to complete homework assignments, to pick up after himself—the way Hank's stepchildren did—and to act respectful and interested. He thought that if Winston would get engaged in one thing, just one thing, his behavior would all turn itself around. Hank bought him books and maps and instruments. Yet, the more Hank gave, the more Winston turned away.

When Winston entered high school, Corrine and Hank had to keep a constant vigilance to make sure he attended classes.

Then, in December, the month he was to turn eighteen, it became clear that he wasn't going to graduate with his class. Hank, who had been painfully patient all along, finally lost his temper, grounding Winston, saying he wouldn't be allowed out after dinner until he passed his summer school class, six months away. Corrine remembered the night clearly. It was a Friday, and they were going out to her department Christmas party. A gentle film of snow covered the ground. It was Ruth's first year in dental school near Boston, and she wasn't coming home. David had already started working, but had used his vacation time to spend the holidays with them. Corrine hadn't planned on telling Hank about the letter from the school until the next day, but he had seen it on her dresser.

Hank had delivered the details of the punishment sadly, the only way a pacifist who spent his life studying battles could. Through the entire lecture, Winston hadn't said a word.

Corrine remembered stepping outside, the thin layer of ice on the steps, taking Hank's arm as they descended. The thick smell of wood smoke from chimneys in the air.

"Maybe, we should stay home," said Corrine, her breath a cloud of white against the dark night.

"No, it's done. He'll finish high school and go to the community college until he brings up his grades. We're not going to run our lives around Winston anymore."

Hank didn't usually care about parties. He often stood by himself looking at the titles lining the host's bookcases, nursing the same beer all evening. Though he liked people and had an easy laugh, he generally preferred to stay home with his own books and family. But that night it was as if he was making a strategic decision. To reveal weakness would bring about a defeat. He chatted and laughed, moving amicably from group to group.

Corrine drank eggnog and talked to a tiny, blond woman—why couldn't she remember her name?—who was up for tenure and trying too hard. Listening to the woman's false brightness, Corrine had been struck by the irony of the moment. Here was this woman, willing to do anything, had in fact done most of the right things her whole life, forced to pander at a Christmas party to a woman who had done everything wrong, couldn't even get her son through high school.

Corrine's conversation with the blond woman was interrupted by Hank. David had called the party to tell them that Winston had taken her car, right after they left. David thought he was just letting off steam and would be back. He hadn't wanted to call and tell on his baby brother. But so much time had passed that he was getting worried.

Hank drove the streets looking for Winston. Then they had sat up all night, frightened about the slippery roads. When he didn't return the next afternoon, they called the police who said there wasn't a lot they could do about a runaway who was almost eighteen unless they wanted to file a stolen car report. They didn't.

❖

Corrine handed the envelope containing her grades to the secretary in the Records Office. She was the only one there, no student workers, no other teachers.

"You know you can do your grades online now," said the secretary.

"I know," said Corrine. "But it was a nice day for a walk."

Afterward she walked over to Hank's office in the history building, stopping at the snack stand to pick up two tuna sandwiches on the way. She knew he sometimes forgot to eat. His door was open a crack, his back to it as he faced the computer screen.

"Anything new on Gallipoli?" she asked, teasingly.

As always, Hank was surprised and happy to see her, as if it was beyond his wildest dreams that he had managed to meet and marry such a person. He was so introspective and studious that he didn't realize he was also charming and desirable.

"Well, I do have a new angle, but it was still Churchill's worst moment."

"Can't you rewrite it?"

He smiled and stood to pull over a chair for her. Watching him, she wondered for the first time if he thought the disappointment with Winston was recompense for his good fortune in meeting her? No, that was the way that she, a critic of fairy tales might see the situation. A historian would analyze a situation based on a complex interplay of the events of the past.

Sitting down, Corrine noticed a photo of Winston on Hank's desk. It took her by surprise. Winston was five or six in the photo. Standing in front of a snowman, he wore a blue snowsuit that she had completely forgotten. His intense blue eyes peered out of the thick fur-trimmed hood. Corrine didn't recall the photo. She wondered where Hank had found it? She had never removed the photos of Winston that were framed around the house, but she had grown so accustomed to them that she rarely saw them. Seeing this photo was like stumbling on a moment in the past, seeing him again at that age, like in her dreams. She never dreamed of Winston as more than five or six years old, never grown up. Often he was lost, in a grocery store or at a playground. She didn't need a therapist to help her analyze the subconscious meanings.

Corrine remembered an afternoon when Winston was in grade school. He had come running in the door, excited about the size of the snowflakes.

"They're as big as daisies. I can see their designs, the six points!"

"How did you do on your math test today?"

With the question, Winston's face had dropped, and he had collapsed on the floor crying, his little shoulders heaving as he sobbed. The sight had terrified her.

"Pull yourself together, Winston," she had said, dragging him up by his right arm.

"I can't do it," he had cried.

"You just need to try harder," she had said.

She had not comforted Winston or even asked precisely what he meant. What couldn't he do? Math? Tests? School? Instead, she had left the room, never even mentioning the incident to Hank. The sight of him, prostrate and crying, had frightened her too much. Had that been her one opportunity, her opening to listen? Maybe she should tell Hank now, let him see her role in the disaster of their son. The anecdote might alleviate some of his own guilt. But she couldn't imagine the words leaving her lips. How was it possible that she wasn't able to share such a thing with the man she loved? What prevented people from revealing such important matters, even as they sat side by side?

They ate their sandwiches in thoughtful silence. Corrine assumed Hank was thinking about the phone call. The night Winston left, they wouldn't have believed Winston would be gone so long. Eight years! How had Winston managed all that time without money or a high school diploma? Just a car that they learned, by a call from the Colorado state police, was abandoned two years after he left. The only thing he had managed to sustain was his absence from their lives.

When Corrine returned home, no more progress had been made on the fence. Instead, the fence maker was striding up and down the far back of the yard, actively assessing his work with his eyes. Pausing at various places, he would look over at what was constructed so far, as if trying to see what the completed fence would look like from every angle. Corrine thought of "Bartleby," a story she had taught a hundred times as an example of an adult fairy tale, and then she dismissed the idea. No, unlike Bartleby, the fence maker preferred to finish his work. It was just that he was having a hard time doing it.

❖

The next day Hank finished his paper and was home early. He seemed ready to celebrate until he learned that the fence maker hadn't been there all day.

"Is it going to be too late for planting if we wait longer?" asked Hank.

"No, no," said Corrine, not wanting him to feel more culpable than he already did. "We still have time, but why don't we drive out to the nursery anyway. Maybe we'll find something we can put in now, before the fence is finished."

Corrine knew what she wanted the moment she saw it—a Forsythia bush, in full-bloom, with a thousand tiny bright yellow, oblong flowers, like little ribbons tied closely together along the branches. It made her think of the last time she had felt lighthearted, on her bike ride past the bed of daffodils.

"We can put it at the far end, an anchor for the garden. It will be easy to leave enough space for the man to finish his fence."

She could tell Hank was happy to see her so happy. Together, they carried the magnificent plant, its roots and soil bound in burlap, to the hatchback. At home, Corrine boiled pasta while Hank dug a wide and deep hole near the end of where the garden would be. She stirred in pesto, and then let the mixture cool. After they planted the Forsythia, they would have cold pasta, bread and a green-leaf salad dressed with vinegar and oil.

Ruth called while Corrine was rinsing the lettuce. Corrine listened to her talk about her patients, a particularly difficult root canal that she had had to refer to a specialist, and the new sofa that she and her husband, a podiatrist, had bought the weekend before. They didn't have any children. They planned to start their family in two years, when they could afford a larger house. When she hung up, Corrine went outside to help Hank sink their purchase into the ground. They ate dinner on the back porch so that they could watch the affect of the sunset on their flaming new bush.

❖

The fence maker wasn't there in the morning when they got up.

"I forgot to ask, what's his name?" asked Corrine.

"Doyle, I think it's his last name, but I don't know for sure, just that that's what everyone calls him, Doyle," said Hank who was meeting a friend in the park to play chess, a reward for finishing his paper and getting it in the mail. "Maybe he'll be there and I can talk to him about the fence, tell him we don't expect it to be perfect or anything. Encourage him a little." Corrine felt a twinge in her chest, a slight pain.

"Why don't you give him some money for what he's done so far?"

"I already did," said Hank. "Do you think that was a mistake?"

"No, no, I'm sure it doesn't matter, his problems are his problems, no matter what we do."

They both grew quiet. She hadn't meant her words to carry a double meaning, but that's how they came out, leaving them both to wonder if they were true.

Corrine spent the day getting her home office ready to work on a paper. The only academic project she had planned for the entire summer, the paper was a rather complex analysis of fairy tales inherent in contemporary film. At noon, when she went into the kitchen to fix her lunch, Corrine glanced out the window. She didn't notice him at first; his dirty clothing camouflaged him against the soil. Then, as her eyes played on the flowering bush, he almost seemed to take shape before her eyes. He was sitting beside the Forsythia, hunched over, beneath its fountain of arching branches, his slumped back to her. He was weeping. She could tell he was crying by the way the wings of his bony shoulders lurched up and down. His elbows were tucked at his sides as if he had his head in his hands. Corrine didn't want to watch, but she couldn't pry her eyes from him. She didn't know how long he had been crying before she spotted him, but she knew he cried for a full ten minutes afterward. When he was done, he stood, dusted off the thighs and rear of his filthy pants, and started walking toward the street, coming down so firmly on each foot that it was as if he believed the sureness would prevent his long body from toppling over. Corrine sprang to her purse, pulled out three twenty dollar bills and ran from the house after him.

"Doyle! Doyle!" she called. He turned to look at her.

"I want to pay you," she said and thrust the crumpled bills into his right hand, hanging at the end of the long arm folded at his side. His eyes were red-rimmed, his face splotchy. He didn't look at the money, just slipped it in his pocket and turned away, embarrassed. Corrine knew he would not be back.

She went inside, looked up Home and Garden Supply in the yellow pages, phoned, and asked if she paid extra if someone could come out immediately and finish their fence that very day. She described the type of materials they had purchased and the three posts that were already in place. If possible, she wanted the fence up before Hank came home. She said she was willing to pay any amount. But even as the words issued from her mouth, Corrine knew that no amount could do the things that had not been done, and undo those that had.

Each of Edge's five children had been fathered by a different man. The first one she had married at age 19 in a ceremony attended by 500 guests, bridesmaids in salmon-colored gowns, and a reception that included chorus after chorus of Champagne corks popping. After that, she hadn't bothered with marriage. And after Jay, father of her youngest, she gave up on men entirely.

Edge, short for Margaret Edgerton, met Jay at the Lucky Links where her oldest boy, Marston, had Saturday golf lessons. At that time in the seventies, golf was still considered a game of the establishment. But Edge wanted her children to have a variety of skills and she imagined a sort of Zen wisdom in golf. Her vision was reinforced by assertions that she overheard Jay say to Marston, like "You have to let go of power to create power."

Watching Jay instruct Marston was one of the few times Edge was able to get time by herself. Her oldest, Alice, probably too young legally to babysit—though more than mature enough in behavior—watched her then-youngest, Ernest, while her other daughter, Robin, spent the day with her father.

Edge sat under a willow tree reading while she ate a lunch of organic chicken on homemade bread and drank freshly squeezed lemonade from a jelly jar. She usually only spoke to Jay at the beginning and end of each lesson, but noticed him throughout—what he said and how he moved, his hands on her son's bony elbows. Jay's face had burned and tanned so many times that his skin reminded her of tree bark, brown peeled away to reveal gold, then peeled again to deep scarlet. The mixture of colors enhanced his green eyes. Veins wound down his arms like heavy electrical cords charging the muscles in his hands that clutched the club. He was her type, Edge thought, though she wasn't certain what her type was, given that the fathers of her children had been so physically different from one another. The first, her only husband, had been a blonde and freckled fraternity boy; the second, a University of Chicago graduate student in Mathematics from India; the third, a local folk singer; and the fourth, a married black dentist. Yet in a way she could sense, but not articulate, they were all the same.

In August, Edge told Jay that Marston would have to miss his last lesson because a repair man was coming right as the lesson ended, and she would neither be able to stay through the lesson or pick him up.

"Where do you live?" Jay asked.

It was what she had hoped he would say.

"North Racine." Edge fingered the tip of the thick single braid that she wore strung over one shoulder. She wasn't able to look him in the eye. His gaze unnerved her.

"He's my last lesson that day. Lots of vacation cancellations. I could swing him home."

"Sure, if it's not out of your way," she said, and—not waiting for an answer—wrote her number on the tiny pad made up of discarded paper scraps she had stapled and kept in her purse.

When Jay dropped Marston off, Edge was impressed that he made no comment about either the number of her children or their varied shades of color. He stayed all afternoon, helped her make dinner, wash the dishes, and put the children to bed. Afterwards, they drank beer on the back porch of the two-flat that Marston's father had helped her purchase before returning to India and the new bride his parents had selected. Edge and her brood lived on the second floor; she rented the first to two young men who helped her with the shoveling in the winter and mowing the front lawn in the summer. Edge and Jay sipped quietly. Like most Chicago back porches, Edge's slanted down, away from the house, to keep rain water from collecting where the porch met the house, rotting the wood. Beyond the porch railing, the sky glowed pink between the buildings across the back alley. With all the streetlights and neon, it never turned completely dark in Chicago.

"I can read out here at night without a lamp after the kids go to bed."

"No kidding," said Jay. "By the way, this is great beer. Full and light, but with . . . a taste I can't identify . . ."

"Nutmeg," said Edge. "I brew it myself."

"You what?" asked Jay.

"I make the beer in the basement."

"No kidding."

"Come on, I'll show you," said Edge. She led him down the stairs to the basement, pausing to show him her backyard, which she had divided in half. On the side that received sun, she grew vegetables. On the shady side, she had made a play area for the children: a huge sandbox that she had filled (and kept full) by having each child carry two plastic buckets of sand back from Lake Michigan whenever they went to the beach; a multi-chute slide constructed from used car parts she had found at the junk yard, including a well-waxed fender she had pounded out; and, finally, a wading pool slightly larger than the sandbox. She had mixed and poured the cement herself and decorated the pool's rim with the smooth sides of colorful broken pottery she had saved.

Jay stared at her, amazed.

"You did all of this yourself?"

Edge glowed with pride. Although many people expressed astonishment, she was delighted anew each time. She was proud of her resourcefulness. But it was more than that; she found intense pleasure in making use of odds and ends—as if determining how to avoid waste was a puzzle she needed to be continually solving. And she did need to save money. After Marston was born out of wedlock, her parents had cut her off. Her babysitting and work at the co-op would not have been enough without her ingenuity and prudence.

"Well, I did get some help digging the hole for the pool from friends and my downstairs tenants."

"But, still . . ." his voice trailed off.

"The play area pays for itself because of my daycare business. Cut rates for friends. Nothing that has to be licensed or anything. It's really just babysitting."

Jay stood in silent awe when Edge showed him her basement: the mini-brewery, the potting area with the wheel and kiln, and the carpentry section where she stored tools, as well as an assortment of lumber she collected from forays around the city.

Later, when they made love on the back porch, they did so with their feet on the downward slant so that Jay had to push with his bare toes to propel himself back up inside her. Edge had never made love on her back porch before. She found the slant titillating. It was as if she had to pull and clutch her vagina to keep him from slipping out and off the porch. He pushed, Edge pulled, each push and pull bringing her closer to losing herself until she got into the rhythm of it—to the brink and back, to the brink and back. It became such a pleasant form of work that she forgot it would eventually end until—upon Jay's final release, he slid out so unexpectedly and completely that—like a flash flood, Edge's sensations all rushed out after him in one long, painfully delicious shudder.

Over the next week, Jay told Edge many times how impressed he was with her frugality. He told her that he had always been a frugal guy himself, making do with what he had. In the summers he taught golf in Chicago. In the winters, he was a ski instructor in Aspen. In between, he rode his Harley down to BaJa Mexico to sleep on the beaches, camping along the way. She told him how she had dropped out of college to get married, about the years of waitressing after the divorce. Her parents' retracted support. Now she worked at home or the co-op, a place where she could take her children if need be. She told him about the jewelry and baked goods she made and sold. He was kind to her children and brought her luxurious leftovers from the country club where he worked one day a week. He seemed happy when the children piled onto his lap. She started to think that maybe he was different from the fathers of her children. Perhaps there was a binding force between them.

"Too bad you're so tied down," he said on Labor Day. "Or you could come with me to Mexico. I've got three weeks after I wrap up here before I need to head for the mountains."

"I could come," said Edge. "Why not? Robin could stay with her dad, and the other kids could stay with friends. It would be good for them to experience some independence without me hovering."

Edge had been anticipating the trip for a while. The rent from the guys downstairs paid the mortgage, and she would have no problem finding someone to replace her at the co-op for three weeks. She had shut down the daycare center before. She had just needed Jay to ask.

The first three days on the road were perfect, the steady vibration of the bike beneath them, the wind in their faces. When they stopped for gas, she checked dumpsters for items thrown away without being unwrapped, stale bread, cheese with mold that could be cut away. Edge liked to make their provisions stretch as long as possible. She showed Jay a way to make fires using fewer matches, and which food scraps could be saved. Coffee grinds were good for scrubbing out the skillet. Unlike Chicago, the nights were so dark that the sky was salted with stars. She imagined bringing her children west to visit Jay in the winters, him living with them in the summers.

In the day, she enjoyed watching the changing landscape shoot past. And she loved to rest her cheek against Jay's back, feel the hum of his body. It was a more complete and intimate form of communication than she had ever experienced. But on the fourth day, when they hit the northern part of the Baja peninsula, she felt some tension. Jay seemed to be giving her the silent treatment. Of course they never actually spoke when they rode, but she sensed a difference. His back was stiffer. That night they set up camp on the beach a little south of Ensenada. Jay was quiet through dinner. Afterwards, he crouched before the fire, poking it with a stick as he stared into the flames.

Edge wrapped up the bread crusts and asked what was wrong.

"That," he said, pointing at her hands with the stick. His face was under-lit by the flames, giving him a mean look.

"What?"

"Bread crusts, you're saving fucking bread crusts."

"They're perfectly good, we can use them for breakfast tomorrow."

"That's not the goddamn point. The point is your total lack of spontaneity. We don't need to save every fucking scrap—we didn't even buy that bread to begin with. Feed the shit to the goddamn birds! Throw the crusts in the water and make a wish! I don't care, just don't save every scrap. I'm scared to go to sleep at night—worrying that you might cut off my hair and weave it into a basket."

Edge felt her eyes well up with tears. She was not the weepy type, but his attack was unexpected.

"I'm sorry. I thought you said you liked my frugality."

Jay tossed the stick in the fire causing a flurry of embers to rise. He stood and dusted his hands.

"No, I'm sorry," he said and stepped around the fire to take her in his arms. "I really am sorry. I shouldn't have blown up. It's just that the way you make use of every last thing is starting to bug me. Just lighten up a little."

He undid her braid and forked his fingers through it, loosening the plait.

"Everything doesn't need to have a use. Some things can just be for fun. Or because they taste good." He licked her cheek and pulled her to the ground. He lowered his voice. "Or because they feel good."

He had strong and gentle hands. As he slid her jeans down over her hips and entered her, Edge remembered him telling Marston "Just guide the club, don't force it, let the ball find the hole on its own." They made perfect love in the sand. The movement of their bodies digging them into a crater. It was the slowest and most erotic lovemaking they had experienced since that first time on the slanting back porch. Edge wanted to hang onto Jay. She wanted to do whatever was needed to make him look at her again with awe.

The next day was better. Jay's back felt pliant and communicative again. Edge rested her cheek against it and watched the scenery fly past. The rocky shore was magnificent; in some spots, waves crashed against the rocks so hard that they shot thirty feet in the air. When they stopped for lunch, Edge made a show of calling each of her children at their separate lodgings and talking without regard for the fact that it was long distance. But the following day, the tension surfaced again. She couldn't stop herself from collecting useful items on the beach. And it was unnatural for her to throw away food that was still edible. She felt Jay's resentment grow with each prudent move she made.

When they reached the outskirts of Cabo San Lucas, they met another couple, Shelly and Carl, who were also camping on the beach, and the tension eased again. Edge didn't like them much. They were a couple of rich kids down from California to surf, both with white-blonde hair, almost ten years younger than she, which made them closer in age to Jay. But they did provide a distraction, a buffer for the tension. Shelly let Jay borrow her board while she hung out with Edge. Shelly was worse than Carl—spoiled and high all the time—but Edge was glad that Jay had a playmate for a while, so she tolerated Shelly, showed her how to string beads and tiny shells to make exotic necklaces and earrings they could sell in town.

Edge had seen a shop that she knew would be happy to purchase her jewelry. She twisted wire and strung shells and talked about her children while Shelly said things like, "Wow, four kids, I can't believe it, you look so young, wow, you make me feel like I haven't lived at all, wow." Edge made four pieces of jewelry to every one that Shelly made. When she saw that Shelly was getting bored, Edge asked Shelly to drive her into town in Carl's van. That way she could go to the shop on her own and Jay would never know she had used her resourcefulness to replenish her funds. She would tell him they had gone to buy supplies. But just as she and Shelly finished changing for town, Jay and Carl came running up the beach.

"Hey, Edge, Carl knows a great restaurant in Cabo. We're going out to party!"

Edge felt her heart sink. Restaurant? Except for a few roadside stands, they prepared all their own food. And the way he used "party" as a verb troubled her. Lots of drinking. She could imagine the expensive sort of place Carl would know. Her resistance must have shown on her face.

"Don't worry, Edge, my treat," said Jay, his voice laced with sarcasm.

"No, no, it's not that. I wasn't worried about money. It's just that food tastes so good and fresh outside."

"Then this place is perfect, it's got a courtyard patio," said Carl. His wet blonde hair, plastered away from his face, had a greenish cast, as if he spent as much time in pools as the ocean. "We can smoke some Cuban cigars, man." He gave Jay a playful slap on the shoulder.

"Cool," said Shelly. "And I can have lobster!"

"What do you say, Edge?" The plea in Jay's tone suggested a final test.

"Of course," said Edge, wondering if she could find a way to slip over to the shop she had seen, make an arrangement to sell her stuff so cheap that it wouldn't have to be on consignment. "If that's what everyone wants. But I insist, I pay for my own."

◈

Broad steps led down into the elegant stone patio with eight tables covered in pink cloth and adorned with deep pink napkins. On two sides of the patio were French doors leading into other parts of the restaurant. Lush magenta bougainvillea draped the far wall in the back. The only lighting was provided by three enormous, dripping candelabras. At most tables sat florid male tourists in pastel golf shirts beside slender wives wearing bright dresses to show off their tans and frosted hair. Edge knew the place was expensive before she even opened the menu. She smiled as a waiter pulled out her chair, the wrought iron feet scraping against the stone floor. With sheer determination, she maintained the smile after she opened the menu and quickly translated the prices. Even with the favorable exchange rate, they were ridiculous. She could feed her entire family for a week for the cost of one entrée. But she would not balk. She didn't know where her relationship with Jay was headed but she didn't want it to end because of one meal. She decided to order the Pollo Monterey. It was modestly priced, but not the cheapest on the menu—so she wouldn't draw undue attention to herself.

"We'll start with a bottle of wine," said Carl when the waiter returned to the table.

"Oh, I don't know," said Edge. "I got so much sun today. It probably would do me in."

As soon as she spoke she felt Jay's eyes on her.

"But I suppose one glass would be okay." Her eyes quickly scanned the menu, landing on a French white she knew from her waitressing days. She couldn't believe her good fortune—it was over fifty dollars in the states, but only ten dollars here. The place had missed its best opportunity for gouging tourists.

"Here's a good one," she said, pointing it out to the waiter before anyone else could speak.

Jay looked skeptical.

"I remember it from when I used to waitress. It's excellent."

When the waiter returned, he poured Edge's glass first. She pushed it to Carl on her right. He swirled his glass, sniffed, and sipped.

"This is nice," he said. "Crisp and dry."

With Carl's verdict, Jay seemed to relax. They toasted one another and fell into story telling. Carl bragged of his trips to Hawaii, the fantastic waves, of the medical school he would attend in the fall. Shelly told of the year she took off from college to travel Europe, of how high she racked her father's credit cards before he put her on a strict allowance. Jay talked of blizzards in the mountains, a daring ski rescue he made. And Edge talked of her adventures around Chicago with her children. Her stories got the most laughs. She knew how to make a trip to the farmers' market with four kids sound as entertaining as Shelly's Champagne boat trip down the Seine. Edge felt her cheeks grow warm from sunburn and wine. But more importantly, she felt Jay's eyes on her—in admiration. She was back in his good graces, back in control, without having to sacrifice too much. One slightly expensive dinner. She was even glad to have Shelly there. Though Edge was older than Shelly, she knew she compared well to her—she was smarter and prettier. More solid. And now Jay could appreciate her sense of economy without thinking it prevented her from enjoying life.

Carl lifted the empty wine bottle dripping from the bucket.

"Who's ready for another?" he asked.

Edge's heart barely lurched.

"Why not?" she asked and laughed.

"Which kind was it?" asked Shelly opening a menu left on the table.

"That one," said Edge, snaking her hand under Shelly's arm to point.

"You're kidding?" said Shelly. "It's a hundred dollars."

"No, ten," said Edge. "You're reading the numbers wrong. The French Chardonnay."

"No, I'm not, it's one hundred. Look," said Shelly passing the menu across the table to Carl. Carl's eyes opened wider as he located the wine.

"Shelly's right. It's a hundred bucks."

A silence descended. Edge could feel her eyes welling up

Jay chortled. "Come on, man, you guys are joking, right?"

"No," said Carl. "All these zeros are crazy. Anyone could make the mistake. Don't worry. I've got a credit card."

"No way, man, we can pay our half," said Jay.

Edge felt she would burst into tears if she spoke.

"Really, it's no big deal," said Carl. "This is my old man's treat—he's so happy I got into medical school, he's not gonna complain about a few extra dollars."

"Yeah, forget it. Let's just enjoy the meal. We can work it out later," said Shelly.

"I am so sorry," said Edge. She knew her voice trembled.

"Don't worry, babe," said Jay. He cupped her hand with his. It was the first time he had called her babe. His voice sounded weary, but tender. She was relieved he wasn't angry. Still, she felt foolish. The dinner had been going well—Edge couldn't believe she had been so careless.

"Hey," said Shelly. "Snap out of it, Edge. It's only a bottle of wine. We've got to get the mood back. Hey, I know—I've got a game we can play. Confess all the people we've slept with. Whoever has the most wins."

"No way," said Carl. "That's a dumb chick game. Guys don't even remember everyone they've balled."

"Come on, try it," said Shelly. "I'll start. Two in high school."

She paused to count on her fingers and squint into the distance as if she was picturing them walking down a gangplank, counting each as he jumped off.

"Seven in my first year of college. That was a crazy year. Nine in Europe. Three when I came back to school. And then you. That makes twenty-two!" She smiled at Carl.

"Now what about you?"

"I told you, I'm not playing. It's a stupid game."

Edge tended to agree with Carl. It was juvenile. But it was taking her mind off the wine and Jay seemed to be enjoying himself. Besides, Edge felt her answer would impress him.

"My turn," said Edge.

"This ought to be good," said Jay, sitting back in his chair, smiling affectionately, ready to hear the tales of the slightly older, more mature woman.

"Five," said Edge.

"No, really," said Jay. "If you're going to play, at least be honest."

"That's the truth," said Edge. "Five."

"Hey, you're making me feel bad," said Shelly forcing a mock pout. "I thought you'd have way more since you're older and were part of the hippie scene."

"No, five," said Edge, still smiling, loving the surprise twist.

"But," said Jay. "You said all four have different dads. I thought . . ."

"Those four and you."

"Whoa, man," said Carl.

Edge was confused when Jay's face blanched a pale green. She reached across the table, but before her hand touched him, he jerked around and gagged. A thin trail of reddish, corn-dappled puke stretched to the floor of the elegant patio. He wiped his mouth with a napkin. He didn't really throw-up, just a slight up-chuck.

"Gross," said Shelly. "Good thing we didn't have more wine." Then it became clear—that Jay would see her lovers as an ultimate form of economy. No man, no sperm, wasted. Even Carl had recognized her error before Edge had seen it.

The ride back to camp was silent. In the morning, they started north without even saying goodbye to Shelly and Carl, who had paid the restaurant bill. Jay's cold back was too stony for Edge's cheek, so she rode with her face in the wind, trying to blink back tears. They made it to Colorado in two days, where they split the cost of her airfare to Chicago. At the airport, he kissed her on the cheek avoiding the intimacy of eye contact, though they both knew it was rather late for him to be cautious. She thought they both must be picturing it—the sperm swimming up the slant of the porch, burrowing itself in her egg. For a second as she boarded the plane, she thought she knew how he was like the fathers of her other children, how they were all the same. The sudden insight flitted across her brain in total clarity. But before she could capture and process it, the revelation was gone for good.

The trip was destined to be a disaster, Stuart thought as he looked at his older sister, Gail. She had lodged herself in the far corner of the Buick backseat. Her oval face was set in a scowl—all her features coming together in an ugly wrinkle. Her long legs, appearing even longer in tiny green shorts, were twisted around one another, entwined like rope. He knew that she wasn't mad at him; they were closer than any of the brothers and sisters he knew. Being, at age twelve, both the oldest and wisest child in their neighborhood, Gail was a leader of sorts, an organizer, and she always made Stuart her second-in-command. But still, her anger, her worry, was disconcerting. Something terrible had happened with their family, an incident that involved their uncle, Travis—Gail's favorite relative—something so horrible that instead of making their usual trip from their house in Columbus to their grandparents' summer house in South Bend, they were going to a bungalow their uncle had rented on Lake Michigan. Gail was angry at their mother for not telling them what had happened, what was wrong.

To top it off, Stuart's parents were arguing. They had started on the porch, behind the morning-glory-covered lattice, and had edged their way toward the Buick. Now they were moving within earshot, his mother opening the car door between herself and her husband.

"He's my brother. I have to go to him," said Stuart's mother.

"Movie melodrama," said Gail almost hissing under her breath.

"What about some loyalty to me? He's my brother-in-law. How do you think I feel?" said Stuart's father. "I'm the one who got him the job."

"I've already apologized for that. So has Travis. What do want from us, blood?"

"Oh God," said Gail.

"Even your parents, Travis's parents, agree with me," said Stuart's father.

There was a silence. Stuart could see his father's shoes beneath the open door of the car. They were black and had designs, swirling little holes, on the toes as if they had once been soft and someone had decorated them with the tip of a toothpick. His briefcase was standing, crooked, next to them on the gravel driveway.

"So," Stuart's father finally said. "That's your final word. You're not going to change your mind?"

Stuart couldn't see his mother's head; it was above the car door opening.

"If I don't go now, we'll lose him forever. I can't change my mind."

The briefcase rose, disappearing behind the barrier of the door. Then Stuart's father's face appeared in the window, next to his mother's khaki-clad hip.

"You kids have a nice vacation. Be good in the car, and when you get to Uncle Travis's, do everything your mother says."

Then, before they could reply, he was gone, his gray-suited back walking away from the car, across the lawn, up the street toward the bus stop.

"Rob, are you going to phone?" Stuart's mother called after him. He didn't turn around, just shrugged his shoulders. Stuart's mother waited until his father had vanished behind a cluster of tall shrubs, then got in the car, slamming the door.

"You mean we're not even going to talk to daddy the whole week?" asked Gail, her face becoming even more distorted.

"Don't worry," said Stuart's mother, stretching her arm along the top of the front seat, looking over her shoulder to back out, "he'll call."

Despite the state of his family, Stuart was excited. This was his first vacation any place besides his grandparents' summerhouse. His mother had said the beach would be right in Travis's backyard and they could go swimming every day. There would be new places to explore, maybe a cave or big gnarled tree where he could construct a fort. Even his premonition of disaster, his curiosity about Travis, was exhilarating. If only he could persuade Gail to share his excitement, everything would be fine.

Stuart stared at Gail, willing her to look at him, to speak. When she didn't respond, the rhythmic movement of the car began to make Stuart drowsy. He closed his eyes, yet didn't succumb completely to sleep, instead remaining in the place between wakefulness and dreaming, thinking of Gail and Travis. He remembered when Travis and his new wife, Margie, had lived with them, for what seemed like a year, before Stuart's father had gotten him a position at his company. Stuart could recall Uncle Travis and Gail in the sun room, seated on wicker stools, leaning over the chessboard. Travis was teaching the game's intricacies to Gail, her face as contorted in concentration then as it was now anger. Her arms had looked particularly slender in the big blue shirt she was wearing; the one Travis had given her with Chinese characters on the back. Travis had pretended the letters read "kick me" in Chinese. Stuart could remember Travis, laughing, chasing Gail, also laughing, feigning attempts at kicking her. Then he imagined his father joining in the chase, his mother, Margie, the entire family running through the living room, weaving in and out of chairs, trying to kick each other, and he knew that he was asleep.

When Stuart woke up, Gail was reading a book, her features almost smooth again. Stuart's mother looked, the way she always did clutching the wheel, small and nervous. Stuart's neck felt stiff. He had been sitting straight up.

"Gail, do you want to play the license plate game?"

She gave him an annoyed glance. "Jesus Christ, you're almost nine. Why do you want to play that stupid baby game?" Stuart felt hurt, struck. He could almost envision, in his mind's eye, pink finger marks, remnants of a slap, embedded on his cheek.

"Gail, try to be pleasant," said Stuart's mother. "I'll play, Stuart. Do you want to start?"

Stuart could see nothing out his window except Indiana plates. He knew they had gone west from Columbus, and were now headed north to Michigan.

"No, I guess I don't want to play. How long have we been in Indiana?"

"We've been out of Ohio for hours," said Gail.

There was no use trying to talk with her. As close as he and Gail were, Stuart knew that she had dark moments, "moods" his father called them. Stuart was sorry this mood had extended to him, but she would get over it. She always did, coming into his room late at night, presenting her secret thoughts as peace offerings. Perhaps, Stuart thought, he could woo Gail by questioning their mother about Travis. Stuart knew very little about the trouble. The only words from his parents' fights that had remained distinguishable, after traveling upstairs, were his father's shouts of "loser" and "liar." He knew his grandmother had argued with his mother over Travis, his mother had even hung up on her, but no one had talked to him or Gail. Maybe, Stuart thought, if he began with innocent questions, he could carefully lead his mother to reveal the real trouble.

"Is Aunt Margie bringing the baby?" asked Stuart.

"No," said Stuart's mother without turning her head, offering more.

"Is she leaving him with her parents?"

"Margie's not even coming, dummy," said Gail.

"Gail," said Stuart's mother. "Uncle Travis and Aunt Margie are having some problems. They're not any of our business so it's best we don't talk about them."

Gail was sucking her lower lip, as if considering whether or not to pursue the subject. Stuart felt guilty, ashamed; Gail's concern was obviously real, painful, while his had only been a curiosity, a ploy.

"Hey," said Stuart's mother. "I bet you two are hungry. Stuart, do you want to reach up in the cooler and get some sandwiches? There's some Orange Crush, too."

Stuart shifted to his knees and leaned against the back of the front seat. He bent forward and flipped open the lid of the red and white cooler. There were six sandwiches wrapped in wrinkled tin foil and six cans of Orange Crush sitting on a bed of ice.

"Do you want anything, Mom?"

"No, I'll wait until we stop."

"Gail?" He tried to make his voice sound casual, less urgent than he felt.

"No... well, maybe just a sandwich."

Stuart selected two sandwiches and a can of soda, feeling icy in his palm, and reached forward to pull the lid closed. He slid back down, his leg brushing Gail's thigh as he handed her a sandwich. He moved back to his window and peeled the foil from his sandwich. It was egg salad: cold and a little wet. It tasted soggy. Stuart smiled at Gail; he didn't want to wait for Gail's nocturnal peace offering. He wanted Gail's comfort now. She didn't return the smile; she was no longer sucking her lip; instead she was staring at the back of their mother's head, her unwrapped sandwich on her lap.

"It'll be a cold day in hell before we see Margie again," said Gail.

There was a silence. Stuart couldn't believe it, but their mother was ignoring Gail's remark, pretending nothing had been said. Then, as if in slow motion, Stuart saw Gail's sandwich fly up. He didn't think she aimed it, but the sandwich hit their mother's head over the right ear, then separated into individual slices of bread. One slice, spread with mayonnaise and a few clinging pieces of egg landed in his lap. He felt the car swerve. Everything seemed to go colorless for a second, a blur, then the car was still on the shoulder of the road. His mother was screaming.

"Out. Gail, get out of this car."

Opening and slamming their doors, Gail and his mother slid out, moved around the car until they were facing one another. His mother leaned forward, hands on hips, lips moving fast, yellow and white flecks in her hair, her polo shirt collar flapping in the breeze created by the rush of traffic. The sound of passing cars obscured what they were saying, but when Gail climbed back inside, her eyes, looking as hard and clear as glass, had tears forming in their sharp corners.

◈

Sullied darkness, like overlapping screens, was beginning to form as they reached Travis's neighborhood.

"I think this is the street," said Stuart's mother, stopping and balancing a sheet of directions on the steering wheel.

"Where's the beach. I thought Travis said the beach was in his backyard?" asked Gail.

Gail had begun talking an hour back, submitting short challenging remarks, as if testing their mother.

"I'm sure it's close by. 'In the backyard' is just an expression.'"

Stuart's mother turned down the street. Sheltered by trees were tens of little cottages, bungalows: pink, blue, green and yellow. There were pink flamingos, plastic, poised on single legs in most of the yards. Some of the lawns had posts holding silver balls. Stuart noticed a ceramic squirrel, affixed with wire, darting up a tree.

"This place is really tacky," said Gail.

"You know Travis is down on his luck. He can't afford beach front property."

"He should have tons of money," said Gail.

Their mother stopped the car.

"What do you mean by that?" she said, looking over her shoulder, her raised eyebrows pushing her forehead into folds.

"Nothing," said Gail, glancing away.

"All right, Gail, but I'm warning you for the last time. This has got to stop." She turned her attention back to the road and began driving again, slowly, checking the house numbers. "Here it is: the green one with the big rock in front."

After they were in the driveway and began unpacking the trunk, Uncle Travis emerged from the house. He was a big man with a broad face. His cheeks ballooned even larger above his thick beard, as if a shave would release constricted flesh, swelling his face still more. Stuart imagined pricking a cheek with a pin, watching the air seep out, then winced and ran his tongue along the soft lining of his own cheek.

"Meg," Travis called, spreading his arms wide. Stuart's mother ran from the car into his hug. Stuart and Gail followed, trailing their bags. When Travis freed their mother, he stood over them, beaming.

"So, how are my two favorite kids?"

"Where am I sleeping?" asked Gail.

Uncle Travis's face seemed to drop, his broad cheeks and smile melting into his beard. "You and Stuart are in the room to the right—the one with the two cots."

Gail slung her bag over her shoulder, tossing both braids back and walked to the house. When she had disappeared inside, Stuart's mother and Travis looked at each other.

"Does she know?" asked Travis.

"Only things she may have overhead. She's confused right now, but give her time—she'll get over it."

"How about mom and pop? Are they over it yet?"

Stuart's mother looked down at him, smiling. "Stu, why don't you put your things in your room—explore the house."

"But I want to talk to Uncle Travis."

"We'll have plenty of time to catch up later, little buddy, a whole week," said Travis. "There's a garden house in the back. Why don't you check it out? Maybe you could make it into your own little fort."

"I don't do forts anymore," he answered, feeling acquiescence, now, would be a betrayal of Gail.

"Stuart, Uncle Travis and I want to talk. Go inside; we'll be along in a minute."

Stuart dragged his bag toward the concrete slab steps, intentionally going slowly, wishing they would begin talking again.

❖

The thin single mattress on Stuart's cot sank in the middle when Stuart lay down, creating foam walls on either side of him. He felt trapped in the center. Their room was only slightly bigger than the storage pantry at home; there was an inch of water in the back yard and the entire house was wet and smelled of mildew. The evening had been awful. Gail had started a game of chess with him, but had gone into their room to read before they had even finished. She had said little to Uncle Travis, answering his questions with laconic utterances. And it was obvious that his mother and Uncle Travis were just waiting for him to go to bed so they could talk. He could hear them talking now, only the clarity of their words muffled by the flimsy walls.

When Stuart had come to bed, Gail had pretended to be asleep, but he knew she was awake, even now. Her steady breathing gave her away. He wished she'd come sit on the edge of his bed, talk, mend the unpleasantness that had occurred between them earlier in the car.

"Gail," he said toward the dark space dividing their cots. "What do you think Uncle Travis did to make everyone so mad at him? Do you know?"

He wanted to sound sincere, transform his curiosity into concern as real as hers. But there was a short silence before she spoke, and, when she did, her answer was perfunctory, just a string of words not completely reflective, Stuart felt, of her thoughts.

"No," she said. "I heard daddy say what Travis did; the word was something like 'imbecile,' only longer. It has something to do with money and daddy's office."

"Maybe Travis acted like an imbecile at work, embarrassed daddy." Stuart was happy to be conversing with her, offering a suggestion.

"No, the word wasn't imbecile—something longer."

"Maybe..."

"Shhh," she breathed. "They're saying it now."

Stuart heard the flutter of Gail's sheet as she tossed it back and rose from her bed. Stuart sat up. He watched her dark form move to sit cross-legged, by the glowing yellow crack beneath the door. In the faint light, he could see the space between the pajama top and bottom, the way her elastic band dipped, exposing the curvature of her back bone. He sat very still until, finally, she stood and returned to bed.

"The word is 'embezzlement,'" she said, almost as if she were thinking aloud, talking to herself. "He took thousands and thousands of dollars from daddy's work and kept them in the bottom drawer of Aunt Margie's dresser." A thief. Uncle Travis was a thief.

"Did Margie know?"

"She had to," said Gail. "The money was in her dresser."

"Why did he do it?"

"Because everyone at daddy's work was stupid. Travis said everyone, even daddy, was unfair."

"What did mother say?"

"Just that Travis should have waited. Everyone liked him— everyone always likes him—he would have gotten a promotion eventually." There was an odd toneless quality to her voice. "She said he wouldn't have been a clerk, doling out expense money forever."

Stuart felt her interest slipping, receding into her thoughts. He wanted to prolong the conversation. "Did Travis..."

"Stu," she said. "Let's just go to sleep."

When he finally slept, he dreamed of an enormous bureau drawer filled with dollar bills, a confusion of green paper surrounding stacks of neatly folded blue shirts with Chinese symbols on the backs.

Stuart was the last one up. The bungalow's main room was divided into a kitchenette and a living room. Stuart's mother was standing at the sink in the kitchenette side, washing dishes. When she saw him, she removed a hand from the water to pass him a yellow plastic plate with toast and two wrinkled strands of bacon.

"Where is everyone?" asked Stuart.

"Uncle Travis went to see if he could buy you and Gail some rafts."

Would he steal the rafts? Stuart imagined Travis running from a store, two huge inflated rafts tucked under his arm.

Later at the beach, policemen would arrive to retrieve the rafts. Stuart envisioned himself floating, saw the darkened trousers of the police as they waded in after him.

"He didn't have to do that."

"He wanted to do something special for you and Gail."

"Where's Gail?"

"Outside," said his mother, indicating the window with a tilt of her head. "Look, she's already found a friend."

Stuart took a bite of bacon, the tip crumbling on his tongue, sending a little tremor through his system, and looked out the window. Gail was siting on the big rock at the driveway's end, wearing her yellow terry cloth bathing suit cover, with white spaghetti shoulder straps. A fat boy in a T-shirt and bathing trunks was standing next to her, talking.

"Who's he?" asked Stuart, knowing immediately that he didn't like the boy.

"He lives down the street. He said he'd take you and Gail to the beach."

"Why does he have to take us? He's no older than Gail," said Stuart. He wanted to be alone with Gail to talk about Travis.

Stuart's mother turned around, wedging her soapy palms behind her on the counter. Her eyelids were swollen as if she hadn't gotten much sleep. "You're not going to start giving me problems too, are you? He's not really taking you—just showing you how to get there. Uncle Travis and I will meet you there in a little while." She paused. "Now finish your bacon and go get into your suit."

❖

After Stuart had changed and started outside with the towels, he noticed that the boy was even fatter than he appeared from the window. His T-shirt rode up over his belly creating an expanse of flesh shaped like a gigantic eye, his naval a blinking pupil.

"This you kid brother?" The boy asked. His eyes were small and moist like fish eggs.

"Uh-huh," said Gail. "Stuart this is Chuckie. You ready?"

"Yeah."

"Okay," said Gail. "Let's go."

Stuart walked down the road two paces behind them. Gail always managed to do this: find friends who would do as she wanted. But usually they were not fat kids like Chuckie and usually she let Stuart share her power. He didn't think her slight now was intentional, only a result of her preoccupation with Travis.

"Look at the crap everyone has in their yards," she said as they passed a lawn with a flock of pink flamingos.

"My parents have some Dutch people and a windmill," said Chuckie.

"Well," said Gail, sucking her lower lip as she paused to retie a strap on her freckled shoulder. "That's different. A windmill is different."

They walked along the water; tiny waves lapped the edge, leaving dark imprints that quickly faded, absorbed by the sand, only to be replaced with another imprint. Stuart attempted conversation, but found his uncompleted sentences left hanging, ignored. Gail was too obsessed with Travis, Stuart assumed, to answer. Chuckie was too occupied with Gail, probing clumps of seaweed with a stick, reciting legends of the beach—a ring he'd found when diving, his school friend who'd died after walking out on the ice last winter—barely suppressing his glee at the slightest response from Gail. Chuckie would have gone mad, absolutely crazy, Stuart thought, if he had met Gail at her sharpest, when she wasn't preoccupied.

When their mother and Travis arrived, Stuart abandoned his efforts at conversation to join them on the towels, lending, with some relief, his new raft to Chuckie. His mother and uncle helped Stuart build a sandcastle with a drawbridge, little shells as windows and dried seaweed for hedges. Gail and Chuckie, dragging their rafts, staged three walks in front of the castle. Each time, Stuart felt less enchanted with the sand, the drying seaweed. He wondered if Gail had confided to Chuckie about Uncle

Travis. Later, when they started home, Stuart wasn't surprised to see Gail's mood had changed from detachment to darkness. Her features amassed, again, in the center of her face, her shoulders hunched forward as she walked. Stuart tried to stay between Gail and his mother, prevent a dispute. Yet as soon as Chuckie left their group, Gail accused their mother of being rude to him, creating little dust clouds as she stamped her foot in the road. The argument was inevitable. But Stuart was surprised that his mother's punishment—not allowing Gail to go out to dinner with them—was so harsh. He was even more surprised that Travis remained silent, didn't try to intercede on Gail's behalf, the way he always had when he had lived with them. Stuart felt worse than he had in the car the day before, even worse than he had when he was alone with Gail and Chuckie. At the restaurant, he stole mints from the cashier's station, planning to give them to Gail to cheer her. But when they got home, his mother announced that Gail was already asleep. "Probably for the best," said Uncle Travis.

❖

Stuart awoke to darkness. He knew he wouldn't be able to return to sleep. Everything in the room seemed damp: the foam mattress, the walls, his hands. He felt sick recalling the day's events. But at least now, he thought, Gail would see that Uncle Travis isn't so special. After seeing him not stick up for her, she'll know not to worry about him. Stuart reached beneath his pillow for the mints, and rose from his cot. The concrete floor felt wet and slick beneath his feet.

"Gail," he whispered, sitting next to her on the cot. She didn't answer; but her silent breathing indicated that she was asleep. "Gail," he said again, "wake up." He pulled back the sheet and felt for her shoulder, but found a wad of cloth. Gail was gone! Only a pile of clothing, arranged like a body, remained. Stuart's throat seemed to drop, slip through his chest as he went to the open window. The moonlit backyard was empty except for the garden house: wet and empty, a long lake, short shoots of grass protruding like reeds in a pond. The mints slipped from his hand. Stuart's throat pulled tightly shut. He wanted to cry out, but he couldn't. If he told now, he would lose Gail forever. But what if Gail was gone for good? He started for the door, then heard a noise, a soft creaking, in the yard, and turned back to the window. The garden house door was opening. Gail and Chuckie came out, their bare feet sunk ankle deep in the watery grass. Stuart watched as Chuckie kissed his sister, his fat stomach pressing her against the garden house wall. Stuart walked backwards to the bed, sitting down, watching the window, waiting. No more than a minute could have passed before Gail appeared on the window ledge, crouching, her long legs, silhouetted against the moon light, making her appear like some type of monstrous insect.

"Gail," Stuart said, surprised by the breathy quality of his voice.

"Stuart! What are you doing up?" She said, seeming to spring to the floor.

"Waiting for you. Where did you go?"

She sat next to him on the bed, still wearing her yellow bathing suit cover. Her slender shoulders looked especially fragile in the pale light.

"I was just mad so I went out for a while. Nothing seemed fair. But I'm all right now. Are you mad at me?"

"No." He thought he should return to his own cot, but he felt too shaky to stand.

"We better go back to bed now before mother or Travis hears us," she said.

"Okay," he said, rising carefully, his knees still feeble.

"Stuart," she said as his leg touched his cot.

He looked back. Her oval face was half shadowed. The eye on the illuminated side seemed larger and brighter than it ever had before. "You're not going to tell."

"No," he said.

◈

Early in the morning, their father called. When Gail came out of the bedroom to talk Stuart was surprised to see she was wearing her blue shirt with the Chinese symbol. As Gail took the phone, Stuart watched Uncle Travis to see if he would notice. Travis took a sip of his coffee, a few drops clinging to his whiskers. Then he smiled. He waited until Gail was off the phone, then, as she passed his chair; he kicked her, tentatively, from behind. Gail giggled. Her face looked guileless, as if there had been no estrangement between her and Travis.

The four of them, with Stuart and Gail balancing rafts on their heads, started for the beach early, before the neighborhood showed signs of movement. Stuart's mother lifted her shoulders and sighed as they left the driveway, still happy from talking to his father.

"Even the street seems prettier," she said, looping her arm through Travis's.

Stuart looked down the street. Yes, it did look prettier, woodsier. Then something caught his eye, the only trace of bright color, a yellow and white windmill straddled by two Dutch people. The raft slid from his head to the road, as he stood staring. No other artificial color along the road.

"I've got to go back," said Stuart.

"What?" asked his mother.

"I've forgotten something. Just go ahead. I'll catch up."

He left the raft in the road and walked quickly up the driveway, around and behind the bungalow, his feet squishing in the saturated grass, to the garden house. He pressed his thumb beneath the rusted hook lock and jarred it loose. The door fell open, casting a shaft of sunlight across the only room of the house. There was a confusion of color: pink flamingos stacked against one another, on top of each other, ceramic squirrels and silver balls piled at their feet. He only looked for a moment before closing the door, relocking it. But as he gazed at the bubbled and peeling paint on the door, he realized his mind's eye had registered details—the scratches on a silver ball, the tip of a flamingo's crooked beak, black as if dipped in paint, and the solitary eye of a ceramic squirrel, looking up at him.

His lungs felt heavy with the water that had warped the door and clung to everything else as he remembered his sister's eye— so bright in last night's moonlight. He started back across the yard, slowly at first, then began to trot, run, his toes slipping backwards in the water, as if he might not be able to catch up— as if he had already lost her.

After Greg's arrest, I searched my memory for clues, signs that I might have missed. I think we all did. Greg was nerdy— dressed a bit avuncular for a guy in his early thirties, cardigans and wide corduroy pants—but not so nerdy that you could consider that a factor. He had sharp eyes and an easy smile, though the space between his upper lip and his nose bowed in a way that gave him a slightly simian appearance, a goofy trait that softened the intensity of his eyes before the arrest, a feature that seemed somewhat sinister after.

Greg was a mathematician who had apparently held real promise in his youth. The newspaper account said that he had earned his bachelor's from M.I.T., his Ph.D. from Stanford. The article also mentioned an important proof he had developed in his early twenties. Since I'm a painter, a portraitist, I know little of these things, but I vaguely remember hearing about it when he was hired. He was considered a good catch for our small Ohio college. We have a respectable reputation in the arts and some of the humanities, but math and science are not among our strong suits. The article on the arrest said Greg was 32, unmarried, and lived on McKinley Street. I know the block; located in what we call faculty ghetto—where the younger associate profs live—it is composed of smallish wood-frame houses, dormered windows on the slanted roofs, many with wide front porches and neat gardens.

He seemed skilled in conversation; not that I could recall actually engaging in a one-on-one with him (believe me, I have racked my memory) besides the usual perfunctory inquiries about one's health. Though he was not in my department, we served on the college retention committee together before his arrest. One time he supported me in advocating for reduced class sizes even if it meant an additional class for faculty members, a somewhat unpopular issue. For this I felt grateful.

Our committee met at 8:30 a.m. on Wednesday mornings and, as is the custom at our college for meetings scheduled before nine, breakfast items were served. I noticed he avoided the healthy fare (bran muffins and fruit) in favor of coffee and a single glazed donut. He had a slight paunch, a bulging above the belt, though he certainly could not be called fat. After the arrest, the image of his donut—the crusty glaze, the puffy central hole, sitting in the middle of the small white paper plate with fluted edges—acquired a sinister symbolism in my mind, much like the space between his nose and upper lip.

During the week the news broke, I was happy to leave campus right after my office hours each day. A van and a news crew had set up residence at the entrance to the parking lot. A few reporters had approached faculty. We received an e-mail from the administration asking us to refer questions to the media relations department. And though the spoken speculation among my colleagues was low-key, it was always present that week, right under the surface, a head-achy drone. We all had more questions than answers. How could he? What could possibly spawn such urges? We are generally a sympathetic bunch, liberal and compassionate, but it was difficult for anyone to muster more than a meager note of sympathy. I think we could have rallied a bit if his preference had been for teenagers, even adolescents. But toddlers and infants? I didn't know such predilections existed. Even Stan Lebowsky, the most radical among us (who before the rubble of 9-11 stopped smoldering, already referred to the terrorists as freedom fighters) wasn't able to mutter more than the word "tragedy," though he did question the administration's right to suggest we not answer reporters' questions.

I didn't see Rachel until Wednesday that week. When I got home from school, she was already in her room, the door closed. She had been at her father's since Sunday night. Though I have primary custody, David and I have pretty much allowed her to spend her time at whichever house she wants since she turned thirteen, almost three years ago. The only real rule about relocating was that the parent in the home she left alert the other of her departure, and the other confirm her arrival. (I had received an e-mail at my office from David and I would reply now that I heard the music wafting from her room.) We trusted her. She was a good student and seldom broke rules, though lately she had seemed secretive, going to her room immediately upon arrival, appearing distracted during dinner, and offering only a half-smile and laconic response if I asked a question or relayed an anecdote from my day.

I wondered if I should have a conversation with her about Greg Campbell. Colton was a small town and an article had appeared in the Colton Courier that day (though at the college, we had all read the news in *The Akron Beacon Journal* on Monday).

I rapped gently on her door, and then pushed it open before giving her a chance to respond. I could see straight into her bathroom, where she stood over the sink, wearing just her bra, scrubbing a green cloth under the facet.

"Just thought I would check in and say hello."

She jumped around and stood in a way that seemed to be blocking the sink, almost as if she was hiding something. "What are you doing?" I asked, taking a step closer.

"Just washing my blouse. I spilled some milk on it."

"Do you want me to throw it in the washer?"

"No, no, this is fine," she said, still blocking my view of the sink. "Daddy told you I was coming, didn't he?"

"Yes, he e-mailed. I was surprised you stayed so long at his house."

His place was cramped and her room there was small, a curtained off section of David's office. She rarely stayed there more than two nights.

Rachel shrugged noncommittally. She was a pretty girl, might even be a beauty some day. She had her father's dark hair and eyes, but my pale skin, which she had not, as I foolishly had as a teenager, sunburned, tanned, sunburned, and tanned repeatedly, coating it with baby oil every hot summer day. Hers was alabaster and flawless. The girl had never even had a pimple. Her eyes had heavy, sensual lids—again, like her father —and her lips were full. She wasn't frowning but her lips seemed farther down on her face, almost as if they were about to slip from her chin, and fall off. With her shrug, I noticed for the first time that her hair was longer than usual, hanging past her shoulders. (It was better shorter, framing her cheeks.) Even more startling was the realization that it seemed dirty, stringy and a bit greasy. She was usually meticulous regarding her grooming and hygiene.

"Lorraine had to go out of town, so I helped dad with the twins."

Lorraine was my ex-husband's third wife. He had been married briefly after our divorce, when Rachel was seven, to Virginia, the woman who had broken up our marriage. He and Lorraine got together a year after that divorce. David and I had tried briefly to patch things up in between his two marriages but I couldn't trust him. I had not had a clue about Virginia until the morning a gym membership for her arrived at our house. David had bought me the same Hanukah gift that he had gotten Virginia for Christmas—gym memberships—and the gym had confused the mailing addresses, including the personal notes from David that accompanied them. His message to her was sexual, and alluded to a "hot" time they had recently had at a conference. They were both in the Creative Writing Department (only six full-time faculty members). After their divorce they had remained friends, almost as if they had never had an affair, marriage, and divorce. Handling such a thing with such little contention is unusual at a small college. Liberal arts colleges often contain more adversarial relationships than other workplaces. I think that is because, unlike at most jobs, where an affair, a fight, or a political coup results in one of the parties leaving, tenured faculty seldom leave. The golden handcuffs theory.

Of course that wouldn't be the case with Greg Campbell. He would certainly be fired. The day after the first story appeared in *The Akron Beacon Journal*, all mentions of Greg disappeared from the college website. Reports said Greg had waived his right to an attorney, confessed to something. Hadn't he seen any legal television shows? Guilty or innocent, you always asked for an attorney. Though exactly what he had done was a bit blurry; child pornography was mentioned, along with the word "infants."

Regardless, his confession made it even more difficult for the rest of us. We weren't able to say "innocent until proven guilty" while we processed the story and came to accept it.

"That was nice of you. Daddy didn't mention it, Lorraine leaving, I mean." Why would he? It was an e-mail.

I thought, again, fleetingly about mentioning Greg, sitting down on Rachel's bed and calling her over for a conversation. When she was young, David and I had prided ourselves on being progressive parents, able to discuss anything with our daughter. In fact, we had talked to her about pedophiles and sexual predators before she started kindergarten. But the story about Greg felt too disturbing. *Infants.* Rachel had been mesmerized by David's twins when they were newborns; she talked continually about the size of their fingers and toes. She found them less appealing now that they ran about and had little tantrums, yet she would connect them with the story. I didn't want to plant the images in her head.

"I made some lentil soup over the weekend. I thought that we could have that tonight, along with some salad," I said.

"That sounds good," she said, still standing at attention in her bra, though she turned slightly, as if to suggest she wanted to return to her scrubbing in the sink, thus signaling the end of our conversation.

"Do you want your door open or closed?"

"Closed, please."

When had exchanges between us grown so formal? And hand-washing her own laundry? Usually, she stuffed it in the hamper without a second thought. Could excessive politeness or taking responsibility for her wash constitute warning signs?

Ridiculous. For what? I told myself I should just be relieved that she had been at the sink rather than at her computer. Who knew what was skulking out there in cyberspace? The F.B.I. had seized Greg's computer. Apparently that was how he had exchanged photos with others with similar urges.

As I tore and rinsed the lettuce for the salad, I wondered about Greg Campbell's parents, where they lived, whether they had heard the news on their own, if he had contacted them—or if they were still unaware. Joyce Smithers, my closest friend on the retention committee (actually at the college since Eve Robins was away on sabbatical at the time) said she thought he was originally from California. That didn't mean his parents were still there or even still alive.

I hoped they were dead—of natural causes, of course.

❖

That Friday there was an emergency meeting of the retention committee. We all rushed in late. Few of us taught Friday classes—so we came scurrying into the room at the last minute, scrambling to get off our coats and grab a little food before claiming our seats around the conference table.

The seats on either side of where Greg usually sat were empty. Apparently, people were even hesitant to associate with his former presence.

Kendall Iverson, chair of the committee, took his seat at the head of the boardroom table and called the meeting to order.

"As you all are undoubtedly aware, a member of our committee has left unexpectedly," Iverson began. He did not mention Greg's name, which I had come to see was protocol now; you were free to whisper about Greg in small groups, but not to mention him publicly. Just as his face and credentials had disappeared from the web site, his name had been banished from our lips. "The purpose of this meeting is to elect a new member to replace the one who will not be returning."

"You called a special meeting on a Friday for that?" asked Joyce. "Why couldn't it wait until Wednesday's meeting?"

I liked that about Joyce. Her forthrightness. I wouldn't put it past her to actually say Greg's name aloud if Kendall didn't watch himself.

"Joyce, if you don't mind, we're going to follow Robert's Rules the same as we do at any other meeting." Kendall Iverson had a sparse, crinkly beard that reminded me of pubic hair, the way it curled against his pasty skin. "If you wish to make a comment, raise your hand."

Joyce raised her hand. Kendall nodded in her direction.

"You called a special meeting on a Friday for that?" A few of us tittered. "Are there any emergency retention matters I don't know about? Are students flocking from the college now in response to the unfortunate news?"

All right, so even Joyce could not say Greg's name in a group.

"We have a number of important issues coming up and a new member can't vote on them until he or she has heard them read at a meeting. Therefore, it behooves us to have that member in place now so we will be able to vote the following week," said Kendall. His moist lips were almost unnaturally red and moved in strange shapes in order to firmly articulate the point he was making. As I watched them open and close, into circles and arcs and crescents and oblong squares, they looked almost obscene. A talking vagina. It was at that point that I noticed Joyce had a single glazed donut on her plate. She usually had a muffin. The room felt overheated. My sweater—though it was soft cashmere—itched.

What had Greg Campbell thought about as he sat among us in the retention meetings—smaller class sizes, learning groups, creating a greater sense of community, or how he planned to satisfy his impulses? His exterior competently concealed what went on inside his head. The news had broken five days ago; we had had an entire workweek to absorb it, yet the information only seemed to be sinking deeper into our sub-consciousnesses— our secret thoughts of the secret thoughts of the man who had sat among us. I felt slightly nauseated and pushed my plate away. I had taken only one bite of my muffin.

It turned out that Kendall already had two recommendations for Greg's replacement from the dean, both of whom (women, one with a baby and the other with grandchildren) had already agreed to serve if called upon. We elected the grandmother and were out of the boardroom by 8:40.

"Do you want to get a drink this weekend or see a movie?" Joyce asked. "Bob's going to be in New York."

A few years younger than me, Joyce had soft curly red hair and skin that had taken on a pinkish cast a year or two earlier, when she turned forty. It wasn't an unattractive ruddiness. More like a mild sunburn that brought out her huge green eyes, which she framed in thick banks of false lashes, uncharacteristic of most English professors (or most non-celebrity women in the current century as far as I could tell). When she blinked, I was reminded of doll eyes. She and Bob had been our closest couple friends when we were married. They had stopped talking to David for a while when he was with Virginia. But now I felt certain that they socialized with David and Lorraine, though Joyce never mentioned it.

"I don't have any plans. Just let me check first with Rachel, see if she is going to be with me or David this weekend."

I returned to my office to check my messages. An e-mail from the dean announced a special counseling session "for any faculty or staff members who have been adversely affected by the arrest of a former member of our community. A similar session will be held for students and announced on student sites." The message irritated me in a jittery way, though I couldn't say why. Certainly a counseling session was the responsible thing to do. David and I had gone before our divorce (when I learned of Virginia) and then with Rachel afterward. Partly it was the lack of Greg's name (again) and partly the wording. Did they think there were people who hadn't been adversely affected? But my reaction was more complicated. I felt stumped by what, besides platitudes, counselors would say in such a situation. People are not who they seem; your colleague/professor was just a more extreme case than usual. Should people examine the images the news had conjured in their minds or banish them immediately? Greg Campbell's crime was dark and secretive. It wasn't even clear what exactly he had done: engage in traffic of photos alone or had he also engaged in physical acts? We didn't know the exact extent of the tragedy other than the fact that Greg Campbell's life—at least as he had known it—was most certainly ruined. Whether he had hurt others, whether he went to prison or not, whether he killed himself or not, his life as a professor who sat on retention committees and ate donuts supplied by the college was certainly kaput. His acceptance at M.I.T., his years of work on his dissertation, his pride at the proof he had developed, all his little kindnesses to others, mattered not.

I lifted the phone to call David. I knew he wrote on Friday mornings, but always answered if Rachel or I called.

"What's up?" he asked after obviously seeing my name on the phone's display panel. I imagined his eyes were now trained back on the computer screen. He had had a long dry spell—six years since his last book, which had sputtered and died quickly.

"I just wondered if you knew Rachel's plans for the weekend?"

"No, isn't the ball in your court now?"

"If Lorraine is still away. . ."

"Lorraine? No, we came back last weekend."

"You came back? You all went, even the twins?"

"Of course, the twins. Didn't Rachel tell you? Lorraine's mother took a spill, so we all piled into the car on Saturday afternoon. Lorraine just needed to get her set up with a caretaker. Got back Monday night . . . hey, if you're upset that I left Rachel alone . . ."

"No, no, I must have misunderstood something she told me." "What?"

"Oh, nothing, but, I was wondering . . . has she seemed different to you in some way lately?"

"How?"

"Oh, I don't know, more secretive." It would sound silly to cite her greasy hair and washing her blouse. And it might sound like jealousy if I questioned why she spent more time at his house recently. Telling him her lie about helping him with the twins seemed like tattling. So, I was left with no examples, waiting for David to fill the space.

"Well, she was pretty shaken when Tom dumped her, but that was over a month ago," said David.

"I never thought they were that serious."

"Are you kidding? That kid practically lived at our house."

This was news to me; he had only been to my house once or twice to pick up Rachel. Since Rachel has e-mail and her own cell phone, I had no idea how much they communicated other than that.

"Maybe, I'm just being overly sensitive," I said.

"No problem... hey, how about that guy in the math department? What a creep! Did you know him?"

"We were on the retention committee together."

"Man, what lurks in the minds of men. But what boggles my mind is how he thought he would get away with it, with all that shit on his computer?"

I was tempted to ask David how he had thought he would get away with his affair, with buying two gym memberships at the same gym in a small town, but I knew that would be an unfair comparison. More importantly, I didn't want to sound as if his transgression was still foremost in my mind, as if I remained bitter.

"Yes, well, it's certainly disturbing," I said, making a mental note to search Rachel's hamper for the blouse she had washed.

Rachel stayed with me until Saturday morning, and then announced she was leaving for her father's. I called David to let him know. Lorraine answered the phone. David still didn't have a cell phone, said he didn't want to be in constant communication with everyone in the world. I could hear a screaming toddler in the background.

"Do you want a ride? It's pretty cold outside," I asked Rachel.

"No, I feel like the walk."

David and Lorraine lived a few blocks from Greg Campbell, in the junior faculty ghetto. Right before his affair, David and I had graduated from that neighborhood and bought a Victorian in the full professorship ghetto (on the same street as the college president), a four bedroom in anticipation of our growing family. Large houses are relatively inexpensive in Colton. With manufacturing dying in neighboring towns, the college provides most of the employment besides service jobs. David and I had decided that for Rachel's stability, she and I would remain in the house. David moved into Virginia's house, but once he left her and married Lorraine (who had managed the Italian restaurant in town before the twins), he had had to return to the smaller frame houses in the slightly less fashionable neighborhood. Not that it was a bad neighborhood; besides being a bit shabby, no place in town was unsafe—or at least appeared unsafe on the surface.

The most direct route to David's house passed right by Greg Campbell's house. All this time, Rachel had been walking past his place with no idea of what was going on inside. As I realized this, I had a momentary glimmer of relief that Greg had liked infants, not adolescent or teenage girls. My thought was immediately followed by shame. If I was wishing, why not wish for him to like someone in his own general age group? To distract myself, I went up to my studio, the bedroom with the best southern light, to draw.

Over the Christmas holidays, I had begun a series on famous scientists associated with inventing bombs. I preferred working from live models, but I had had such success—even had a show in New York—with the series I did on radical women writers, all based on photographs, that I had decided that the overtly political might garner me more attention than the subtly political series, like unwed mothers, burn victims, and factory workers that I usually undertook. And, like David, I felt I needed more success. After all, I am over forty now.

Thumb-tacked black and white photos of scientists ran across the top of my bulletin board like a row of wanted posters in the Post Office. I plucked one of Edward Teller from a sixties issue of *Life* magazine, and clipped it to my drawing board. His eyebrows were his most interesting feature, like bird nests pasted above his lids, so many wayward twigs and wild weeds sprouting that it was surprising he could see. My initial pencil studies are always realistic, but when I do the final portraits in paint, they turn abstract. I knew that his eyebrows would somehow figure prominently in the abstraction but I wouldn't know how until I began painting. I had done at least a dozen preliminary studies. He was the type of man that I felt I could sketch forever. Still, once I began drawing his full lips, I found my mind wandering, my drawing mutating—Teller's lips metamorphosing, protruding, bowing out, turning into Greg Campbell's lips.

124

I sighed. Why fight it?

I almost never drew from memory, but Greg Campbell was on my mind, his situation had struck a chord I was having difficulty quieting, so inevitably, he would land up on the paper. I turned the page of my sketchpad, and watched what I recalled of his face take shape, his mouth becoming more like a rictus, his eyes beady and birdlike. I worked until late afternoon, going back and forth between Teller and Greg, until the natural light faded and I realized I should get ready to meet Joyce. The second I pushed the tack back into Teller's picture on the bulletin board, I realized I had not heard from David. My throat constricted in panic. I picked up my cell and quickly punched in his number.

"Hey," he answered. "I was just about to call you."

"She just got there? She left before ten this morning."

"Hey, chill out, she's fine."

"David, you're supposed to call me."

"Come on, she's sixteen. She probably stopped at a friend's. I'll give her the third degree as soon as we hang up."

"No need for that, please don't mention it, just call me as soon as she is ready to leave—and let me know if you and Lorraine are going out of town while she's there. There's no point in her staying at your place when you're not home."

"Yes, captain," he said, one of the phrases he used to irritate me when we were married. I don't think he had said it more than twice since we had divorced.

Before calling Joyce, I went into Rachel's room and ransacked her hamper. I found the green blouse she had been scrubbing. The fabric on the shoulder appeared slightly darker than the rest of her shirt. If milk as she claimed, it would come out in the

125

wash. I pulled out the rest of her clothing—an item at a time—and found two other tops with stains on the shoulder, one had been hand-washed but the other contained dried crud. It smelled slightly of spoiled milk, or perhaps, vomit. I tried to recall the last time I had seen Rachel drink a glass of milk. Bulimia? Rachel had never worried about her weight. And part of the stain was actually on the back of her shoulder.

❖

Colton only has one small, second-run movie house, so that night Joyce and I traveled twenty miles outside of town to the outskirts of Akron, to the nearest mall with multiple screens. I drove. We took back roads. A gentle snow drifted from the dark sky.

"So, did you hear that Greg is back in Colton?" asked Joyce, once we were outside of Colton.

"No?" I felt my gloved hands tighten on the wheel.

"He has to wear an ankle bracelet. He can't leave his house and his father has to stay with him. His parents—they do still live in California—put up their house for bond, and his father moved out here temporarily."

"They're on McKinley Street?"

"Yup. His dad has to be here until the trial. And Greg isn't allowed to use a computer."

"Has anyone from the college talked to him?"

"That, I don't know. I just hope none of the townies bother him."

We were quiet for a while, visually hypnotized by the snowflakes, though my mind hopped from idea to idea. What in the world could Greg and his father do in that house all day by themselves?

"Joyce?" I finally asked. "Do you and Bob get together with David and Lorraine?"

The pause that followed was answer enough.

"I'm glad you brought that up. Because, well, first let me say we never talk to Virginia, and if David and she were still together that would be it. But it's a small department and Lorraine, well, she seems nice enough. Anyways, I've felt a little dishonest not mentioning it."

"That's okay. I understand."

"Of course, I'll never be friends with Lorraine like I am with you. It's a couples' thing. And we never talk about you; you're off limits."

"Really, that's fine. You don't need to defend yourself."

It was interesting how couples were such different entities from singles. How Lorraine and Joyce could socialize as if I didn't exist and Joyce and I could be friends with so little mention of my former husband and his wife. A husband I had talked to three times a day—what to make for dinner, what to do over the weekend, whether to cut my hair an inch or two— until the gym membership arrived in the mail and then, nothing, as if that earlier life had not existed. I remembered how just weeks before the membership arrived, Virginia had brought me a glass of wine at the department Christmas party, sat down next to me, and cozied up to gossip about the department. Her auburn hair had fallen like a curtain to block out the rest of the revelers, making our conversation seem intimate and private. Her eyes were set so far apart that another eye would have fit easily between them. Almost like a bird. Had she been trying to find information or simply titillated by the deception? Prior to the affair, David and his colleagues had all laughed at the way she played up to certain male members of the administration to garner privileges for the department, how she mocked the same administrators with hilariously cruel detachment in private. Why didn't either David or I understand that that sort of dissembling was seldom limited to one area? If I hadn't accidentally received the wrong gift membership, would the affair have fizzled on its own, been a secret I never learned? What other nefarious dual existences didn't I know about? Thank goodness Greg wasn't married.

"Watch for the sign for the interstate," I said.

Was the only difference between Greg Campbell and the rest of us the fact that the spread between his double lives was greater than the distance between our dual lives?

⊕

The following Saturday when Rachel announced she was going to her father's, I was ready. I planned to follow her. I called David before she left.

"Tell him that I might stop at Heather's on the way," said Rachel as she wound her tangerine scarf around her neck and pulled the zipper of her black down parka up the center of her torso. I assumed David had talked to her last week about the discrepancy between her departure and arrival, which had alerted her to the need to create a cover. Hence, Heather.

I watched from the window until Rachel turned the corner at the end of block, and then slipped on my own coat and ran outside. I cleaned snow off my car windows, and drove in the opposite direction of the one Rachel had walked, and then circled back to McKinley Street where I could park a safe distance from where she would enter the block. I knew following her was wrong on some levels, but I tried to convince myself that since she walked past Greg Campbell's house, it wasn't a bad idea to check out the route. I marvel at how I was able to know I was lying to myself at the same time that I imagined I was being a prudent mother.

I beat Rachel by a few minutes. I couldn't remember Greg's exact address but I knew that his place had to be one of three houses. Their exteriors gave no clue as to whether they contained a happy little family, an axe murder, or Greg Campbell and his father. I turned the engine off because I didn't want the purr of the motor or the clouds of exhaust against the cold to attract attention. As I sat there, waiting for Rachel to appear, I wished I had painted her. I had done many sketches of Rachel when she was younger, but never painted her portrait. I liked having the drawings; they seemed more intimate than photographs, but to turn her into an abstraction seemed exploitive. The women artists I admired, like Alice Neel, who had used their children as subjects, never seemed to be very good mothers. But now, I had a feeling I would know Rachel better--what lay beneath the surface of her skin—if I had recreated her in paint. Faces were an abstraction of what lay within. The car was already cold when Rachel appeared, her bright scarf looking like something a hunter might wear for protection in the woods.

I watched her walk. If she continued to Heather's house, she would turn left at the end of the block: for David's, she would turn right. She did neither. Instead, mid-block, she turned into the parking lot of the Congregational church.

She had found religion?

It was disturbing, of course, but almost a cliche. Daughter of liberal professors...blah, blah, blah. As a humanist, I didn't want my daughter to find conventional religion, which I believed was a barrier to thinking deeply. But, at least it wasn't a cult. The Colton Congregational was practically Unitarian. And, I reasoned, as I turned the key to start the engine, if the church offered her comfort at a particular time in her life, it was better than drugs or promiscuity. What real harm could prayer do?

I found myself smiling, as I started the ignition. The moment I did, the door to one of the three houses opened and a man stepped out on the porch. A knit cap was pulled down over his ears and a gray scarf covered his face, yet I could sense it was Greg Campbell. My hands froze. I didn't want to shift the car into drive and call attention to myself. What if Greg recognized me? Would he think I was spying? I sat perfectly still as Greg walked toward me. I exhaled when he stopped at the mailbox at the end of his walk, lowered the red flag, and removed a stack of mail. He was the same Greg outwardly, unaltered by his experience. His movements seemed neither hurried nor purposely slowed. No one hurled rocks or names at him. I wondered if I approached him if we would both pretend nothing had happened, whether he would inquire about my health or the latest actions of the retention committee? I felt relief when he finally disappeared back inside. Just as I put the car into drive, a bus pulled out from the church parking lot. I had forgotten that since Colton had no official bus station, the bus to the Akron Greyhound station made a pick-up in the church parking lot each morning—I hadn't used it in years.

I spotted the saffron scarf through the window behind the driver and shoved the gear back into park, and slumped against the seat.

Why was Rachel on the bus?

It was as if the ground had opened beneath me. I waited until I felt steady enough to drive. I didn't need to hurry. The bus was slow and I knew the three stops on the route had not changed. At each one, when Rachel didn't depart, I would go to the next stop before the new passengers boarded. After the last one, I drove directly to the station and waited for Rachel to arrive.

I sat at the far end of the terminal, in a cold plastic giant eggholder-shaped chair, next to a black man who appeared to be homeless. A sheen of dirt and grease covered his jacket breast, the cuffs of his sleeves were frayed, and he emitted a rancid odor. Rags were tied around his shoes. He kept dozing off, slipping to the side, and then righting himself. I re-adjusted my scarf to cover my nose. I had purchased the cheap navy scarf at the newsstand and wrapped it around my head. The best disguise I could come up with in such short notice with so few resources. I didn't think it would matter. People seldom recognized familiar faces in places they don't expect to find them—just as everyone looks familiar when you are expecting someone. On the drive to the station, I had even begun to question whether the man who had retrieved the mail had in fact been Greg Campbell. After all, I could only see the strip of flesh between his hat and his scarf. It wasn't even clear that he wore glasses. Would the ankle bracelet even allow him to walk to the end of his drive? Yet whoever the man with the mail was, if not for him, I would not have been on the street when the bus left the church, nor would I be sitting in an Akron bus station next to an apparent homeless man, waiting for my daughter to appear.

Rachel emerged from her gate with her head down, her walk purposeful. I followed her at a distance, out the doors, to the left on Broadway Street. Her orange scarf made her easy to follow even at four blocks back. At first the area we walked seemed depressing, gray and a little desolate in terms of pedestrians, but not dangerous given the proximity to the expressway. The landscape changed when we rounded a few corners and began passing boarded up buildings and broken down cars. My heart thrashed in my chest, knowing that in my solitariness I would be easier to recognize if Rachel turned around. I need not have worried. My daughter seemed unaware of her surroundings. She didn't even look up when a Rottweiler lashed out from beneath a collapsing porch, straining his leash to snap and bark.

I had not worn my warmest coat. The new scarf was thin and provided scant protection from the wind. My toes felt like little round ice cubes. I was about to speed up, confront her, when she turned down another street and I saw her bolt up six wide steps of a low-slung building, her orange scarf, in a flash, disappearing inside. The two-story building, constructed of gray-painted cinder block, was beside a small parking lot—with a few old, but workable cars, pulled up to the building like kittens to their mother. Lines of squat windows wrapped both levels like ribbons around a flat package. I increased my stride. The sign above the door said: Harvey Clinic.

Rachel, Rachel, my baby, what was wrong with my baby?

It couldn't be an abortion clinic; she would need a companion for that. They would insist she have a person waiting to drive her home. Maybe a follow-up visit to an abortion? It couldn't be a disease. H.I.V. I would know about a disease. She was too young for tests and diagnoses without parental consent. But what about that milk-like spittle on her the shoulders of the tops I had found in her hamper? A drug addiction?

I counted to five, and then walked up the steps.

My body felt as if it had taken a beating. I opened the glass door to find myself in the reception area. A half dozen sad looking people slumped in two rows of chairs across from a reception counter. Most of them were African American but a few were white, if you could call their washed out fading yellow pallor, white. I walked up to the counter and the youngish African American woman sitting behind it looked up at me. Her skin was the color of pale chocolate milk and a constellation of black moles ran from her chin up her right cheek to beneath her eye. Her face seemed open, as if the constellation was three-dimensional and a tiny winged creature could fly into it. She smiled.

"You here for the holding program?"

My stare must have been blank.

"Your first time?" I nodded.

"Third door on the left, down the hall. You're gonna like it." She handed me a pamphlet. I looked at the cover. Clip art of a grandmotherly African American woman cradling a baby to her chest was beneath the heading VOLUNTEER. None of it made sense. I opened the pamphlet and began reading. My eyes skimmed the words, something about volunteers being needed to hold and cuddle babies with H.I.V. or born with cocaine addictions. I stared for a minute, letting my mind absorb this new twist, and then walked down the hall.

Outside the open door three coats hung from of a row of hooks affixed to a horizontal bar of wood. Rachel's coat, draped by her orange scarf, hung on the end. Soft music wafted from the room. I slowed my pace, moving just close enough to see into the room, while maintaining distance. Three women—my daughter the youngest among them—sat in a row of five bulbously upholstered armchairs of different shapes, across a cracked linoleum floor from a gaggle of cribs. None of the women looked up. Their eyes were all fixed on the faces of the babies in their laps. One of the woman was African American and as grandmotherly as the woman on the brochure. The third woman was probably just a little younger than me; her long henna-colored hair was streaked with wide yellow highlights and she wore a gold ring in her nose. She was so obese that only a hint of her baby was visible in the logs of her arms. None of the babies squirmed or cried. Rachel pointed a bottle into her baby's mouth. Her chair was yellow and brown plaid, a spray of stuffing leaking from an arm's sleeve. I took a few quiet steps closer. I must have been fewer than a dozen feet away. Still, no one glanced in my direction. Though Rachel's face was averted, the gleam of light from the band of windows and the angle at which I stood allowed me to study her features, the softness they had acquired in their strange mix of anguish, ebullition, and ecstasy,

134

glowing and melting together, slipping down the contours of her face like butter. I wasn't sure how such a conflicting group of emotions could exist in one expression.

It was odd that I had never considered that her double life, that anyone's secret life, could be positive. I knew there were anonymous donors to charities, but those people weren't leading actual double lives. They were just writing a check. Why was she doing this?

The question triggered more questions. My mind sped up, zooming from one question another.

Hadn't she received enough mothering from me? Or was it a result of a secret abortion or miscarriage? Or something as simple as David's twins growing older? Why not tell us what she was doing? Could it have had to do with Greg Campbell's name being connected with infants? But surely this started before the news broke. I would never know because I knew that to break the trance, the connection between my daughter and the infant, would be an inexplicably cruel violation. No, Rachel could never know what I had witnessed. But before I turned to leave I wanted to see the baby's face.

I leaned as close as I dared. The little orb of grayish-lavender blankness was cut off along the top by a flap of a pink blanket, so that the brow looked flat, the face the shape of a closed clamshell. The bottle obscured the other features, making the face seem little more than a sucking machine, inflating and deflating as it drew from the rubber nipple, as if trying to pull another life inside as quickly as possible, a life that would multiply and mutate, again and again, in the vacuity behind the mask. The fierce repetitive motion kept me transfixed, locked inside it, as I realized that the urgency of feeding might be one of the last times that the child's outward abandon toward a goal so closely aligned with what was going on inside her head.

APPROPRIATE BEHAVIOR

As she usually did at four p.m., before making tea, Emma Stroberg spread open the crack between the heavy drapes of her front window, and peered out. Her next-door neighbor, Jennifer Wilson, pushed her fancy double-seated baby carriage (with only one wheel in the front, like it was some sort of racing device). The neighborhood had transitioned twice since Emma's arrival. From mostly Polish to mostly Mexican, now to young couples, of who knew what background! Third, maybe fourth generation American. The men had brown hair, neither dark nor light, the women, the same, except for the blonde stripes they added. They only lived in the neighborhood long enough to rehab their "starter" houses in the city before moving to Evanston or to Oak Park for the schools.

Starter—who used such words for houses?

Jennifer stopped the stroller at the bottom of her front steps.

Emma quickly pulled her sweater from the hook by the door and slid it over her shoulders. She wanted to catch Jennifer before she unbelted her children from their stroller. Jennifer always knew the street gossip.

She was one of the few neighbors Emma talked to anymore. When the Wilsons moved in, Jennifer had come to introduce herself. After telling her name, she had proudly proclaimed, "I'm a stay-at-home-mom." Though Emma had felt slapped, she quickly recovered. Jennifer could not have known. And afterwards, Emma noticed the term cropping up frequently, on television, in the women's magazines. "Stay-at-home-mom" seemed the modern way of saying housewife.

Huffing and puffing, thinking how she needed to get more exercise, Emma made her way next door before Jennifer made it inside her house. Her four-year-old sat in the grass while Jennifer unfastened the seatbelt of her one-year-old daughter. Seat belts for strollers? But who was she, of all people, to complain about safety devices.

"Jennifer," she called. "I was wondering, if you know, for what reason is Mrs. Cain moving?"

The FOR SALE sign had been erected across the street the day before, and now a moving van parked in the driveway.

Jennifer swooped her daughter up into her arms. Emma kept her eyes on Jennifer's eyes. She did not look at the daughter.

"Oh, she bought a condo in the city. Took just her bed and moved last week. What's the point keeping a house now that everyone is gone. It's not like she kept it up. "

"She did her best," said Emma.

"Whatever." Jennifer's lips twisted together to signal disagreement. Jennifer's hair looked like it had been pressed with a hot iron. The blonde streaks made it resemble striped tea towels hanging on each side of her face. When Emma was young, she had sprayed perfume on each roller before winding it into her hair to make fragrant curls. "Whatever the reason, I can't say, I'm sorry, Miss Stroberg. That was not a lucky family."

Emma was not really a Miss. She was a Mrs., but after the move from New York to Chicago, she let people assume. Just like in 1947 when she moved temporarily from Brooklyn to Queens, she let people assume she had lost her husband and daughter in the war, not after they had made it safely to America. She knew that she should be ashamed to lay claim to the horrors that had befallen so many others. But who is to say one tragedy is worse than another? A tragedy is a tragedy.

"Her move is perfectly appropriate, given she's by herself. Better to pay assessments and have other people do the work. If she stayed and continued to let everything fall apart, all our property values would decrease."

"Appropriate" was another of those modern words, like "stay-at-home-mom." In Emma's time, it had not been appropriate for a single man and a single woman to travel together. Now that was fine. But everything else was measured in terms of appropriateness. Jennifer had talked for weeks about having appropriate activities at her son's birthday party. Appropriate party favors. She worried how to handle it if someone gave an age-inappropriate gift. Emma had considered saying, "Why not think about fun?" But who was she to give advice? She was just glad that she paid a neighborhood boy to cut her grass and had money for repairs, so nobody could talk about her property values.

"I have something I would like to send her. Do you have for her a new address?"

"No, I didn't really know her that well. But I could ask Ms. Worble at the library. I know they were friends."

"That would be wonderful, if you could ask," said Emma, who sometimes went to the library to look at the free magazines, but didn't know the names of any of the people who worked there. "My kettle is probably boiling. Would you like to join me for tea?"

She would not have asked except that she knew Jennifer would decline. The day she introduced herself was the last day Jennifer had been in her home. Emma preferred it that way. Since she gave up teaching piano years ago, few people entered her house. No one had even asked her about lessons for—how long, she didn't know. Now that time was mostly behind her, it was harder to sort out. Events were a little jumbled, not always clear what came first. Single days seemed endless in her memory, while whole years were forgotten. The last time someone had inquired about lessons, she called herself retired. She had wiggled her fat fingers stiffly and said, "Who can play with this arthritis?" Her arthritis wasn't really so bad that she couldn't teach if she wanted. The problem was that she had grown fat. She couldn't stand thinking of how she would appear to a tiny girl sitting next to her on the bench, her knees squeezed beneath the keys. She didn't want them to laugh, or worse, be frightened of her, think of her as a monster.

When she went inside, Henry and Roosevelt, her two oldest cats, greeted her.

"Hello, boys," she said. "Where's that lazy Einstein? Napping again?"

Her kettle whistled.

As a young woman in Germany, Emma had been petite, slender. Almost too slender. She and her sister, Hilda, had put pencils under their breasts to see who was filling out first, becoming more womanly. Emma's pencils always rolled away, not enough weight to hold them. Hilda strutted proudly around the room, a pencil pointing out from beneath each ample breast.

You should see me now, Hilda, she often thought, I could carry a hammer, two hammers, under each breast. It was hard to believe that these gigantic orbs were parts of her body. Her breasts didn't really develop until she was pregnant. And then they were a nuisance. She remembered that night in the tree, the longest night of her life.

She and her husband, Abe, along with three others, had hid all night in trees, soldiers camped below, just meters away. She straddled a branch, her arms wrapped around the trunk, her breasts painfully spread on either side, her cheek against the rough bark. All of them barely breathed, worried on their separate perches that the others would give them away. Breathless, human fruit. She thought of it years later, in America, when she learned the meaning of that Billie Holiday song on the radio. *Strange Fruit.* No they had not been hung from the trees, they were not dead, but any moment. . . a cough, a sneeze and they could be plucked to their deaths. What a harvest if the soldiers had thought to look up. She had tried to hold in her pee, but she felt it seep through her panties and run down the trunk of the tree. Emma was not sure the underground would have taken her if they had known she was pregnant. Thank God, they—the human fruit—were all young and strong, and that her pee was quiet.

They had waited for hours, frozen in silence, even after the soldiers had long departed. Finally Abe whispered. "We need to go or we'll miss the car." Sometimes she wondered if he hadn't spoken, would any of them have spoken? Or would they all simply have rotted on the branches?

They were lucky, just in time. The driver was about to give up.

"It's not my choice," he said. "They tell me to wait no more than an hour."

The car took them to the banana barge, and the banana barge to Africa. When Emma in her petulance had complained, "Newlyweds, we should be out dancing," her husband had waltzed with her among the crates on the deck, in the moonlight. From Africa, the three others went to South America, she and Abe, sponsored by her Uncle Max, her father's brother, took a boat to New York. Her sister, Hilda, and her husband, a doctor, were already in Queens, just two blocks from the uncle. The uncle found Emma and Abe a tenement apartment in Brooklyn.

"When your husband finishes college, you too, can buy a house in Queens like you sister," said Uncle Max. A house they would always live in, she had thought at the time. Who knew such things as starter houses?

Emma had offered to give piano lessons to help out, but both her husband and uncle had said no, she should stay home and take care of the baby. A-stay-at-home-mom.

❀

In Chicago, in the fifties and sixties, her students were usually forced into lessons by their parents. Few wanted to learn after they discovered how much practice was involved.

Jane Cain was her only student, ever, who sought her without assistance from her parents. When the bell rang and Emma peered out to see her on her porch, she was nervous. Was it a prank? She had seen Jane before on the street and knew she was a wild girl, who cut her own hair and ran with the boys. What if Emma opened the door and she ran away? All her friends hiding in the bushes, laughing, pointing at Emma for being such a fool to open the door. Or worse, what if she threw a tomato in her face? After her third ring, Emma decided she had no choice. Could she hide in her house forever? She opened the door cautiously.

"Miss Stroberg, I would like to know how much you charge for piano lessons?" Her face was handsome with strong cheekbones. Her speech sounded practiced.

When Emma stated her rate, Jane said it was too much and asked if she gave scholarships. Emma had laughed, surprised by the feel and sound of it in her throat. It had been years.

"I'm serious"

"I will talk with your parents. What is your name?"

"No, this is my business. They don't have money for this," she said. "My name is Jane Cain."

"Well, Jane Cain, I suppose we can make an arrangement," she said.

Emma was surprised when Jane showed up at the appointed time and was more than pleased by her determination. The others wanted to learn songs right away. Jane wanted to learn the piano, notes, the sound of each key, how to read music.

As Emma poured tea into the fancy Rosenthal china pot her sister had given her, Henry leaped on the counter and watched the process. He liked to watch the liquid arc from the spout into the cup. He sat and waited for the tea to steep. When she poured herself a cup, Henry stuck his head under the facet to drink. The other two politely drank from their bowls.

"Too hot for you, Henry," she said, the same as she did most days.

Roosevelt made his way to the counter via a jump to a kitchen chair, then to the table top, and, finally, the most treacherous part of his journey, the place where he sometimes slipped, across the gorge between the table and the counter. Unlike Henry, he was too old for a single leap from the floor to the counter.

Emma had tea every day at four o'clock. It was her low period of the day. If she didn't have tea she might fall asleep during the five o'clock news, and what that did to her night's sleep, she didn't like to think.

Emma had just put the kettle on that day, four years ago, when she saw the ambulance across the street. The siren was not on, nor was the red bulb glowing and revolving. The vehicle was deadly still. A small crowd, maybe eight people, had formed on the sidewalk in front of the Cains' house. Emma continued watching as two men carried a stretcher from the house. The body was covered in a white blanket, even the head.

Emma had turned off the stove, found her sweater on the back of a kitchen chair, and walked outside. One of the men in white was closing the ambulance doors. He trotted around to the passenger side of the cab, climbed in while the other started the engine, and they were off. Still no siren. By the time Emma arrived, the crowd was dispersing. She recognized Maureen Kelly, the mother of a student.

"What happened?" she asked.

"Jane Cain killed herself." She continued walking, tossing back more words over her shoulder. "She shot herself in the head."

Even though Emma knew Jane had moved back into her mother's house, it took her a moment to understand who was dead. It was Jane Cain, all grown-up, not her mother. Emma had walked around her living room in circles for hours, didn't watch the news, forgot to feed her cats. Edgar and Franz were the old ones then. Roosevelt still had some spring, and Henry was a mere kitten.

The next day, like all the women on the street, she had taken food to Jane's mother. Luschek kugel. She had also brought her gift, in a package, but the time never seemed right to give it. She sat politely in the living room for what seemed like the right amount of time. People said nice things about Jane and told stories of the people they had lost. Mrs. Cain didn't seem to hear. She was divorced. Jane had been her only child. Emma returned home without ever giving the gift.

Emma thought about coming back later, when no one else was there, to tell her own story and present the gift and provide an explanation. But time, like it so often does, had gotten away. Now, she had to give the gift, before she had lost track of Jane's mother entirely.

❧

There had been a problem with the heat in the tenement from the beginning. Either not warm enough or no heat at all. While Abe was at work in the day and at City College in the evenings,

Emma's hardest job was keeping the baby warm. She would wrap Rebecca in layers of clothing and blankets, then hug her to her breast in bed. Still, the tip of her little pink nose felt like the tip of an icicle. Sometimes Emma would turn on the gas oven, sit in a kitchen chair, Rebecca in her lap, in front of the open oven door. When desperate, Emma went to Mrs. Klein's, the only apartment with a phone, and asked her to call the landlord, but Mrs. Klein always said the same thing, "Already I phoned, twice I phoned, three times. You think I'm just sitting in here like it's Miami Beach? The man should be boiled in oil." So usually, Abe called when he got to work, though they knew it did little good.

"I'm just the service," the woman would say. "I'll give him your message."

When things were good, Emma and Abe joked about it. If one of them asked the other for help with something, they would said "I'm just the service" and laugh. They had a beautiful baby girl. They were young and healthy. Lucky. They had escaped the Nazis.

Friday was Abe's day off. No work or classes. Emma crept around the flat and tried to keep Rebecca occupied until her morning nap so that Abe could sleep. Usually he woke just as she was putting Rebecca down.

On the coldest day of that year, February 18 (Emma would never forget the date), Abe was still asleep when Rebecca began to drift off. Emma didn't want to put her in bed with Abe still asleep. What if he rolled over and squished her. But how could Emma get anything done if she had to keep a sleeping baby warm? A thin layer of frost had formed on both of their windows, making it impossible to see out. Emma scratched a hole in the middle of each pane. The frozen linoleum floor crackled under her feet. So Emma removed the dresser drawer they used as a cradle when they wanted the bed to themselves. She tucked Rebecca inside, and pulled the drawer into the doorway of the kitchen, close to the oven, but not too close.

When Rebecca fell sound asleep and Emma's hands were free, she thought about making a special dinner. Abe liked a good meal on shabus. While everyone was asleep, she could go to the butcher and buy a nice chicken. Chicken tonight and soup tomorrow.

She whispered in Abe's icy ear, "I'm going to the store. Rebecca is asleep in the drawer by the kitchen."

Abe mumbled acknowledgment and rolled on his side, burrowing deeper beneath the covers.

The sidewalks were icy but it felt good to be out, where it was natural for one's breath to make clouds in the air. In the bakery window, she saw a little white cake, trimmed in blue with pink rosettes. Buying it was extravagant, but she wanted a treat on such a cold night. The baker placed the cake in a little white box and tied it with string. Next she bought some new shabus candles. Abe would like that she had remembered to do that. Emma was only half Jewish, on her father's side. He hadn't been observant, seldom went to temple. They celebrated both Christmas and Passover. Abe's family rabbi had refused to marry them because Emma's mother wasn't Jewish. They had had difficulty finding a rabbi who would. Abe's family was not orthodox, but devout. His mother kept a kosher house, and though that seemed too much work, Emma had agreed with Abe to provide their children with a religious upbringing. Or at least, Friday night shabus and the high holidays.

At the butcher's, Emma saw Devorah, a woman her own age from her building. She was carrying her son, dressed in a puffy snowsuit. He was a little older than Rebecca, almost two. Devorah and her husband, Mihael, were the only other Germans in the building. Most of the others were Polish, Lithuanian, or Russian.

Emma and Devorah discussed the heat situation in the building.

"The authorities should be called," said Emma.

"Why bring trouble on the building?" asked Devorah. She was dark-eyed and pretty. "But I can't stand the thought of going back there and cleaning without taking off my coat. On again, off again, all this week."

"Do you need to go back now? Maybe we could have lunch, some coffee?"

Devorah looked at her son who was sucking the melting snow on one of his mittens. Emma felt proud of herself for making such a move. She had heard of American women who lunched. Seen a magazine article on the subject.

"I suppose he can wait a while for his nap," said Devorah. "He's down to only one a day."

They went to a luncheonette where all the food items were behind little glass doors. Devorah had coffee and a sticky bun she shared with her son. Emma had coffee and a sandwich. Emma didn't want to brag, but she couldn't help telling her that she and Abe would be moving to Queens in the spring. They had planned to wait until Abe finished college, but the situation in the building was so horrible that her uncle and sister's husband were loaning them a down payment. Immediately after she told the news, Emma was sorry, ashamed of her pride. Devorah looked sad.

When they walked back into the building, they ran into Mrs. Klein leaving. A huge woman, she wore a green wool tent of a coat and a flowered babushka on her head, earmuffs over the scarf.

"The gas, it went off," she shouted at them, clearly unable to hear her own voice under her head wear.

"Oh, no," sighed Devorah. She looked about to burst into tears. "Not another problem."

"It's back on, an hour almost" shouted Mrs. Goldberg. "So is the heat, but not without three calls from me to his service."

"Thank God for that," said Emma, passing them to trot up the stairs. She had been gone longer than she had planned. She didn't want Abe to be angry. He worked so hard. He shouldn't have to mind the baby on his only day off.

❖

After Jane Cain shot herself, some of the neighbors visited Emma. They thought that since Emma lived directly across the street and had tutored Jane in the piano, she might have more information.

"I hear she was doing drugs and sleeping around. No wonder she was depressed. She looked crazy with those wild blue eyes."

"Who am I to judge?" asked Emma. "All I know is the piano, she played like an angel. And her eyes were green, not blue."

Though she refused to speak ill of her, Emma was angry with Jane. Who would do such a thing on purpose? Wasn't there enough misery in the world without creating it? It was ironic. Emma remembered when she had heard the word the first time. She had thought it meant tragic. She had overheard someone say it about her own situation. Ironic that she should escape the gas over there to get it over here.

※

Emma smelled the gas before she reached her landing, before Irving Katz, the floor below, opened his door and cried, "I smell gas!"

She dropped her packages, the chicken plopping on the wood, the white cake box tumbling down the stairs, the candles rolling after it. Her hand trembled as she inserted the key. She realized that when the gas had gone back on, the oven wouldn't. No one to light the pilot. Just the gas, pouring out of the door left open. Her husband and little girl asleep, as the gas filled the apartment.

Irving Katz rushed past her into the kitchen and tried to open the windows. They were frozen shut. He took her broom and plunged the end through the kitchen window, right in the middle of a hole she had scratched out earlier. Emma stood paralyzed in the doorway.

"Turn off the oven," yelled Irving as he leapt over the drawer that blocked the way to the bedroom. He didn't look inside the drawer as he leaped. She heard him slap Abe.

"Wake up, wake up. Gas!"

Like a sleepwalker, Emma walked first to the oven, switched off the gas, then to the drawer. She looked down. She knew what she saw, but she couldn't process it. Her daughter was in the drawer, but she looked more like a large baby doll, inanimate in its store box and wrappings. A perfect baby doll except for her bluish face and purple lips. In her somnambulist state, Emma leaned down and gently lifted her daughter, and pressed her to her chest. She walked in a circle. Her daughter felt odd, still and cold, not like her daughter at all.

Irving emerged from the bedroom, his left arm wrapped around Abe, under his arm pit, dragging him, ordering, "walk, Abe, walk." Abe coughed. Irving kicked aside the drawer and commanded Emma to leave. He stood aside to let her go out first. As she carried her daughter down the stairs, the blanket dropped away and Rebecca's dangling legs bounced against Emma's thighs, all rubbery, more like a doll's legs, or the chicken she had dropped. At the bottom of the stairs, a crowd waited in the vestibule and outside the front door. They parted to let Emma pass, then Irving and Abe. Irving dropped Abe onto his knees in the snow. Abe stayed on his knees, coughing. Emma kissed Rebecca's hair, a soft and milky smell mingled with gas, and walked in circles in the snow.

She didn't cry until the ambulance came and Mrs. Klein pried Emma's fingers from her daughter to pass the little girl into the hands of the strange man in white. Then Emma wailed. Like an animal, she screeched at the sky, pulled her hair and ripped her clothes, walking around and around in circles.

"Let her cry," she heard someone say.

When the gasman said it was safe, the other women got her back in the building. She sat on someone's sofa, she didn't know whose, Devorah beside her. She hated Devorah. If she hadn't had coffee with Devorah, bragged to her about her new house, none of this would have happened. Emma shivered and Devorah petted her hair. Emma could hear whispers in the hall.

"Who leaves the oven on and goes out?"

"You leave the shabus candles burning, don't you?"

"It's a sin to blow them out."

"Shhh. She might hear you."

At some point in the night, her sister and her husband came to get her. The next day, after he was released from the hospital, Abe came to see her. He told her that no one blamed her, that a petition was being signed against the landlord. Abe did not talk of them living together again. Nor did he talk of divorce. Either possibility was unthinkable. They could not sit at the same table without seeing the ghost of their dead daughter. But Rebecca could not enter the afterlife without her parents' marriage intact.

They were awarded $50,000, a fortune back in those days. Abe refused to take any part of it. Emma didn't want it either.

"You should be a burden on your sister?" asked her uncle. "Her husband with his practice still getting off the ground and a second baby on the way?"

"On that money, you can live forever," said her uncle's wife.

"Buy a house, invest the rest," said her uncle.

Her sister wanted her to buy in Queens, but she didn't like the idea of watching her sister's children grow up. She didn't want Devorah to come and visit her. She didn't want to hear what Abe was doing. She wanted to move far away. She didn't want people thinking she had lost her daughter in the war. She didn't even want people to know that she had had a daughter.

"I have an associate in Chicago, in Skokie," said her uncle. "You can move there; a lot of other Jewish survivors have settled there."

"No, I don't want a Jewish neighborhood," she had said.

She was only half Jewish, a Mischling if she had not married Abe, a full Jew. And she was not, by her definition of the word, even half a survivor.

❖

As she made her tea, Emma decided that Jane Cain's mother was right to move. Emma poured heavy cream into her cup and cut a slice of the rich chocolate cake she had baked two days before. A little sugar with her tea kept her energy level up. Only a smidgen of cream was left in the carton, so she poured it into one of the cat bowls. Einstein rounded the corner, yawning, and went directly to the bowl. Roosevelt joined him. Henry was too stuck-up to share a bowl, so he sat on the table and meowed as Emma ate her cake. Emma imagined he was saying "Where's mine? Where's mine?"

As a matter of fact, Emma thought, she should have moved right after Jane killed herself. What did she need with a ghost in her backyard? And now there wasn't even a person to inherit it. Emma was leaving her house and belongings divided three ways, to her niece, her nephew, and to the home for abandoned felines, providing they took in her own. It was a shame really. Her uncle had helped her invest wisely, and her home, small as it was, was worth ten times what she had paid for it. Her starter home, and now her finisher home. She would have liked to leave the whole thing to her cats, but she could hear her sister's voice calling from the grave. It's not natural, leaving all that to cats. But what did her niece and nephew need more money for? They had more than they could spend in three lifetimes.

Emma decided one more sliver of cake with her second cup of tea would not hurt. What was she saving it for? And she always held off dinner until seven.

Since she moved from New York, Emma had seen her niece and nephew exactly three times. The first was during her fifth year in Chicago when, after being unable to get Emma to come visit them, Hilda and her husband, his practice flourishing, had taken a family vacation to Chicago, stayed downtown in the Palmer House. Emma accompanied the four of them to fancy restaurants and the museums. It would have been a fine visit if not for Hilda insisting on seeing Emma's house while her physician husband took the children to a Cubs game.

"Why so many cats?" asked Hilda the moment she stepped inside.

"Only four," said Emma. "I read about a lady who had fifty."

"In such a small house as this?"

Emma ignored her, quickly showing her everything in the house except the second bedroom, saying it was for storage. When Emma fixed the tea, Hilda excused herself to go to the bathroom. Emma knew Hilda had peeked when she heard the squeal. She came up behind Hilda. Hilda was staring into the spare room. It was filled with dolls, shelves of dolls, dolls in toy highchairs and rockers, baby buggies, at a table with a tea set, three dolls tucked into the spare single bed, dolls standing and sitting on the floor, dolls playing in the closet.

"Oh, Emma," sighed Hilda. "This is not natural."

"What's not natural? It's a collection. You collect china. I collect dolls." Emma kept her voice steady.

"But a woman your age? They're mostly baby dolls."

It was true, there were three Betsy Wetsies and five Tiny Tears. And dozens of other kinds of baby dolls, a few still in their boxes, resting on beds of tissue paper. Also fancy dolls in period costumes that she had ordered from the backs of women's magazine. A Pioneer doll, a southern belle, a Victorian doll. A Little Red Riding Hood and a Cinderella.

"There must be a hundred dolls," said Hilda.

"No," said Emma. There were eighty-two back then. Sometimes she counted them to make sure none were missing.

"It's not natural," repeated Hilda, shaking her head.

The second time, Emma saw her niece and nephew at their father's funeral. And the third was almost ten years ago, shortly before Hilda passed away, when her dementia got so bad that they placed her in an institution. They told Emma that Hilda kept repeating Emma's name. But when Emma arrived, Hilda didn't say anything. She just blinked and licked her lips. Emma sat by Hilda's bed for a few hours, thinking about when they were girls. When she was leaving the place, she noticed a strange thing as she passed the television room. Four of the women sitting in wheelchairs in front of the screen, myopic looks in their eyes, cradled baby dolls in their laps. One rocked hers back and forth.

"What's this?" she asked her niece, Miriam, named after their dead uncle, Myron. "Do you see those women have dolls?"

"Oh, yeah, they gave mom one, too. But I don't think she holds hers. She's not well enough. The nurses said the women like to have dolls to cuddle. It comforts them."

"So, you think that is . . . natural?"

"Oh, absolutely," said Miriam, "Perfectly appropriate behavior for the final days."

There was that word again, appropriate. And "absolutely," that word had been cropping up a lot lately, as if a plain "yes" wasn't enough. Another one of those words whose meanings had changed since her youth. But the memory of her niece's words verified that her planned gift to Jane Cain's mother was appropriate. A perfect baby doll, lips puckered, eyelids with thick lashes that blinked, and two changes of clothing, still all new in the box. She smiled anticipating receiving the new address where she could send the doll.

As she drank her tea, Emma wondered if nursing homes all across the country gave dolls to all the old ladies. Would the stay-at-home-moms on her street need them at some point? To have something to hold that wouldn't grow old, that wouldn't get sick, and, most important, would not die, seemed the most appropriate thing in the world.

Molly would not have guessed that it could last long—her two concurrent lovers, unbeknownst to one another—but, like so much in life, the years crept up on her.

Molly met Nick at gunpoint. She had only been a waitress at High Vanity a few days before they were held up. Robbed. Stuck up. Knocked over. It seemed impossible. Even five years afterwards, Molly could not reconcile the fact that a gun had been held to her head, cold metal scraping her scalp, the assailant's hand trembling violently as he shouted orders at Nick.

"Move! Move it, mother fucker! I said move! Or this bitch's brains gonna fly!"

The metal twitched against her brow's smooth skin as the gunman railed. Molly wanted to tell him to calm down, to stop shaking or he might accidentally pull the trigger and then he'd be in real trouble. But she knew she would sound self-serving. She also wanted to point out that it was just a fluke that she and Nick happened to be near the register at the same time. Nick barely knew her and, therefore, would be more motivated if the gun were held to his temple. Again, self-serving. Besides, her voice might startle the robber, causing his trigger finger to spasm. Her knees felt liquid, yet her thoughts seemed rational, detached. Even later, when she dreamed about the gunman— his pasty, blue-white face, the purplish bags under his eyes—she was simply talking to him, calmly explaining all the reasons it would be foolish to shoot her.

Nick had responded quickly, lifting the money tray to scoop out the large bills hidden underneath. The gunman shoveled the money in a dirty gym bag, and then turned to flee. As soon as he his back was to them, Nick sank to the floor behind the bar, pulling Molly down with him. Instinctively—or so it seemed—Molly collapsed into his arms. When she heard the swish of the door, she spoke into the stiff white fabric of Nick's chef jacket, her lip brushing a cloth-covered button.

"You handled that well. Does this happen here often?"

Clasping both of Molly's upper arms to push her free of their embrace, Nick stared into her eyes. Then he laughed. He had coppery red hair, and freckles so dense that they looked like they had been sprayed on with an aerosol can. He looked the way she imagined a grown-up Huck Finn would look, his laugh loud and hearty.

Molly laughed back. She leaned to the side, her head against the stainless steel refrigerator door. They both laughed and laughed. She freed her right arm from his grip, pressed her palm to the floor mat for support, and laughed harder. Leaning back, nearly hysterical with laughter, she dug her fingers into the deep holes of the commercial mat, sticky from hundreds of sloshed drinks. Tears filled hers eyes. Nick pounded the floor with his fist. Molly coughed with laughter; her stomach hurt. They both laughed and laughed until nothing but a wheezing sound came out.

Later, after they had dealt with the owner and the police, Molly left her car in the lot, and Nick drove her home where they made violent, frantic, and hilarious love on the floor, against the wall, and on her roommate Abby's futon, the only piece of furniture in the tiny living room.

At the time, Molly had been twenty-one, fresh out of college; Nick, sous chef at High Vanity, was twenty-five. Meeting at gunpoint proved a strong epoxy. Five years after the robbery, they were still together. Molly felt Nick had saved her. They were a threesome: Molly, Nick, and life. In fact, there were several threesomes—Molly, Nick, and the phantom gunman; Molly, Nick, and laughter; Molly, Nick, and Death.

The threesome changed when she met Jay, and Jay replaced death. Molly, Nick, and Jay. The robbery and her new threesome seemed connected. If she hadn't been living as an apex of a triangle for so long, she doubted she would have been able to take on the relationship with Jay, without dumping Nick.

◈

Molly had been a communications major in college. She considered High Vanity a temporary position. Falling in love with Nick had slowed down her job search; still, she managed to find a proofreading position at an advertising agency less than six months after the robbery. During her first month, Jay, one of the agency's few clients from New York, had stopped by her cubicle to talk. The following day he invited her to lunch, causing heads to turn. A peon and the biggest client? She could still remember the feel of his fingertips in the small of her back as he guided her through the maze of cubicles, across the lobby, out the door. She felt her co-workers watching through the glass as they waited for the elevator. When they reached the street, she felt breathless. Jay was handsome and slick. His hair was cut in a stylishly scruffy Caesar, combed with a product that made it appear perpetually wet, a solid brunette block striped with comb teeth marks. He wore a form-fitting black leather jacket, as sleek and smooth as the coat of a race horse. Jay, in fact, resembled a race horse: his prominent chin jutting forward, his dark brown eyes always focused and confident.

It seemed inappropriate at the lunch to tell Jay about Nick. After all, it was just lunch. But her supervisor saw it as more than that. By the next time Molly saw Jay, she had been promoted to a junior account executive and they had business to discuss. On their first real "date" (four or five business meetings later), too much time had elapsed. Bringing up Nick would make Molly appear remiss. By the first kiss, it seemed too late to even consider choosing between them. She had been with both of them ever since.

❧

Molly had avoided Math in college by taking an extra Science course. She had been terrible at algebra and calculus in high school—too abstract—but had excelled at geometry. She loved drawing and labeling the shapes, particularly the triangle. Such a simple shape, just three straight lines, yet so complex, creating strange problems and theorems. She remembered the rules. No triangle can have equal sides and unequal angles. Molly could picture Mr. Wite at the board—flowers of sweat sprouting from the underarms of his short-sleeved business shirt—flourishing the pointer to explain. Tap. Tap. Tap. The sum of the three angles is two right angles. Now when images of Nick and Jay flashed across her mind at the same time, she envisioned Mr.

Wite and the screech of the chalk as he labeled the three vertices of any given triangle with their names—Molly, Nick, and Jay—instead of capital letters. Occasionally it became an isosceles triangle with Nick and Jay both equal distances away from her. More often it was a right angle triangle with her and Nick (or her and Jay) close together, the other one at a distant point.

❖

Molly visited Jay in New York once or twice a month. She told Nick she went there on business, which was usually partially true. He only contacted her by cell so she didn't have to answer at inopportune times (she wondered how people managed lovers before cell phones and e-mail?). At home in Chicago, she spent two or three nights a week with Nick—his nights off—at her apartment. He lived above a small storefront theater so they couldn't walk across the center of the floor before eleven without disturbing the performance below. He claimed the low rent, and the large back porch where he grew herbs and spices, compensated for the inconvenience. Besides, he worked most nights when the theater was open.

Neither lover was particularly jealous, but Nick was a little suspicious from time to time. Jay was too confident to be suspicious.

"It's pretty weird," Nick said, after they had finished lovemaking, an evening that they happened to be at his place. Nick had gone home early after cutting his finger to the bone while chopping vegetables. "Most people know their girlfriend's co-workers. I feel like you shut me out of a big part of your life."

"It's not weird, you work nights, I work days—there isn't much time when we're both free. You know the important people in my life, my mom and dad. Abby."

"You know everyone in my life, all the people I work with."

"That's different. I used to work at High Vanity. Besides, I can come in and hang out at the bar—you can't just hang out at the agency, watching me work."

"I could meet you for lunch."

The thought shot a chill up her spine. What would her colleagues think?

"Ha! When do you ever get up before noon? Anyway, my lunch hour is a rush—I usually just eat at my desk."

In her mind, Molly conjured a flurry of rationales, the same way she had at the robbery. If given a chance, she could explain away his concerns. But turning cold seemed a better strategy. She rolled away from him.

"Are you okay? Can I get you anything?" Nick asked.

"A glass of water would be good."

Nick crept around the perimeters of the room, like a bandit trying to avoid being seen, to the kitchen section. She heard him run a glass under the faucet, then saw him creep back. Molly laughed. She always got a charge out of seeing him do the wall-walk. It looked particularly amusing when he was naked.

He climbed back in bed, handed her the glass, reclined beside her and propped an elbow to rest his cheek in his hand. He apologized as he used his free hand to pluck at loose threads from the bandage wrapping his finger.

"I'm just feeling insecure, I guess, things aren't going that great at the restaurant. When everything is okay and I'm in perfect mental health, I don't get suspicious."

Molly wondered briefly if—since his suspicions were actually justified—whether that meant that his mental health was actually worse when he wasn't suspicious? She shook her head to dismiss the confusion.

"You okay?" Nick asked.

"Are you?" she said.

"Well, I would feel better if we lived together."

"Why not?" she asked. "Sounds like a plan to me."

Nick sat up so quickly that Molly tipped her glass, water drizzling onto the sheets.

"You never wanted to before," he said. "What's changed?"

"Well, with Abby getting married this spring, I'll be lonely by myself. But I want us to find a place of our own."

"That's great," Nick said. "Really great. We'll start looking this weekend."

"But we can't move until May when Abby gets married and our lease is up."

"Whatever, that's a good thing about this place—I don't have a lease to worry about. I'm not tied to anything but you."

❖

Only two people knew about Molly's double life. Abby and Molly's mother. Molly would have preferred no one knew, but she needed Abby and her mother in order to sustain the situation. Abby claimed to have no problem with it. She said men did it all the time, so why shouldn't a woman? But Molly did notice that Abby never left her fiancé alone with Molly. Molly's mother expressed less tolerance. Nick had met both of Molly's parents after the robbery. A few months after she began seeing Jay, he wanted to meet her parents. She had met his. Molly couldn't figure out how to explain Jay to her father— even though she felt he would like Jay better than Nick—so she told Jay that she hadn't had much to do with her father after her parents' divorce. Molly told her mother it was only temporary, just until she made up her mind. Over time, her mother's irritation grew. She felt Molly had made her an accomplice. Talk of Molly and Nick moving in together made matters worse.

"How do you think I feel listening to Nick talk about moving in with you, when I know it's not going to happen?" Molly's mother, an old hippie, still wore her unstyled hair past her collarbone. When she confronted Molly, she flung the right flap of the curly mass over her shoulder, clasped her hands on her hips, and waited for a response.

"It could happen, nobody knows what's going to happen," said Molly, with a little smile, hoping to charm her mother. "You always told me not to future-trip."

They stood facing each other, across the butcher-block island in her mother's kitchen, both eating bowls of homemade lentil soup.

"Oh, Molly," said her mother and snorted, tossing her hands up over her head. "I can't believe how much I've spoiled you! You can't do this to Jay, to Nick. You can't do this to yourself. Someone is going to get hurt, very badly hurt."

"You don't know what it's like to love two men."

Molly's parents had been divorced when she was only four years old. Her mother's first boyfriend hadn't appeared until two years later.

"It's partly your fault. I got too good at pretending daddy didn't exist when I was with you, and pretending you didn't exist when I was at his house."

Molly didn't believe her words but she wanted to shift the blame.

"Millions of kids' parents get divorced and they don't live dual lives," her mother said, but Molly could tell from her mother's voice that she had struck a nerve. Molly remembered her mother's string of boyfriends. They would sit at the oak dinner table once or twice a week and either make baby talk to her or—the scenario she preferred—not seem to notice her presence. Talking or not talking: Molly, her mother, a man. Molly at the distant apex until weeks or months into the relationship when the triangle began to collapse and she fell closer to her mother, who pushed the man further and further away until his vertex shot out the door. The other more permanent triangle, the one containing Molly, her mother, and her father, had a slight right angle, making her closer to her mother than she was to her father, but also closer to her father than he was to her mother. When her father remarried, Molly had become a part of yet another triangle.

✦

In her college dorm there had been a nutty boy, Warren, one of those genius nerds who on the advice of an incompetent high school counselor started college at age fifteen. At first he had tried to make friends. A few of the boys had accepted him as a goofy sort of mascot, but quickly tired of him. Small for his age, Warren had dirty yellow hair and mossy teeth. Without his mother to tell him to brush or take a bath, he sometimes forgot for weeks. The boys went from having him do their math homework and answer encyclopedia questions like a trained monkey, to ignoring him, and, finally, to actively ignoring him. They actually pretended he didn't exist, had never existed. They said things in front of him like they wondered why the college couldn't fill the empty room (his room). Maybe, suggested one, because it smelled so bad? Molly and a few other girls told them to stop at first, but didn't persist, and the boys didn't stop, so eventually, Warren did cease to exist. He stopped going to class, stopped leaving his room entirely. When his mother and a school official came to take him away, Molly watched through the crack of her door. She had never seen anything that sad. Her face burned in shame at the mere memory. She had felt so guilty about not doing more to intervene that she had erased the incident from her memory for a long time. She probably wouldn't have remembered it at all if her mother had not begun hounding her about the triangular nature of her relationship. The word made her think of what they had found in Warren's room after he left. Hundreds of drawings of triangles.

When he didn't go to class, Warren sat in his room figuring out the triangulation of his window with the dorm window directly across the quad from him, and every other building on campus. It seemed he was trying to determine his relationship to the world mathematically.

Oddly, within a week of agreeing to look for an apartment with Nick, Jay suggested Molly move to New York. He had suggested it before, but this time he was more insistent and Molly more agreeable. If she was looking for a place with Nick, it seemed only fair that she look for a place with Jay. After all, when she spent Christmas vacation with her mother, she spent Spring break with her father—at least that was what she told her mother when she presented the new turn of events. Her mother simply threw up her hands and left the room.

Since there were few financial restraints with Jay, searching for an apartment with him was fun. During the process, Molly actually believed she would quit her job, move to New York, and decorate the new place before she started job hunting. When they finally settled on a huge space with golden-colored wood floor boards and enormous windows, Molly was ecstatic —until she pictured Nick standing in a beam of light, looking the way he had last summer on his back porch as he offered her a pinch of pineapple sage to sniff. Molly so seldom thought of Nick when she was with Jay—or vice versa—that the image unnerved her.

"No, we can't take this place," she said. The agent had the lease ready to sign, poised on a bare bookshelf. It was their third return trip to view it.

"Why not?" Jay snapped. "I thought you just said you loved it?"

"It has ghosts," she said. "Or at least a ghost."

Upon her arrival back in Chicago that Sunday night, she went immediately to High Vanity to see Nick. She thought that maybe the apparition had been a sign that he was the one she was supposed to be with. She pushed through people waiting for tables to the bar, the very spot five years earlier where the gun had been held to her temple, and asked Ralph, the bartender, to send someone back to the kitchen for Nick. While she waited, she ordered a Paradise, a sweet pink drink served in a champagne glass. It was a sign, the ghost of Nick in New York had been a sign. She looked at her reflection in one of the gilt-framed mirrors behind the bar—High Vanity's red walls were covered with dozens of ornately framed mirrors—and was frightened to see how much she resembled her mother. They both had curly, ginger-colored hair, and large eyes. She looked away just in time to see Nick round the bar, coming toward her, wearing a big grin. She felt relief at the sight of his double-breasted chef jacket, his closely cropped hair (cut to deal with the heat of the kitchen) and his broad smile. She ran to hug him. He squeezed her tightly. Molly closed her eyes as she squeezed back. Nick was the only person who understood her, the person she had faced death with in that very spot. Molly opened her eyes and there—in the mirror over her shoulder—was Jay, staring at her.

She let out a little shriek, blinked, and he disappeared.

"What? What?" asked Nick.

"Nothing, nothing," she said. "I was just thinking of that night. You know, the gun." It seemed a good explanation for her inexplicable outburst.

What was happening? Why couldn't she keep Nick and Jay in their separate places. Could it be guilt? That had never been part of the equation. Nor was bravado. Though she had to admit to an occasional thrill when she pulled off a particularly tricky maneuver or a flawless act of juggling: ending a call with Jay just as Nick came through on call waiting, waving to Jay as he caught his cab out front the moment Nick came in the back door, going to Valentine's Day brunch with Nick and making it to the plane in time to have Valentine's Day dinner in New York with Jay. But the thrill was not from pulling anything over; it was from pulling it off.

"So who are you going to live with when your lease runs out?" her mother demanded. Molly lay, shivering, on her mother's old sofa, the one with the chintz pattern of birds and tangled vines. Molly liked to come home when she felt sick. She had developed chills and a temperature the day after her most recent trip to New York."

"Whoever finds the right place first? The one who's nicest to you that week?"

"Mom, it's not like that. You know I love them both."

"Then why not just tell them? If it's so easy, just live with the both of them?"

"It's not easy and you know perfectly well that that's not what I'm saying. Why are you on my case? I'm sick."

"And I think that's why you're sick, because your behavior has finally caught up with you." Her mother spoke in an even voice, which made Molly feel worse. Her mother had faint crow's feet radiating from the corners of her eyes that enhanced her attractiveness, made her look more sincere and forthright.

"I'm sick because I was on a plane full of sneezing people, and I just want some peace and quiet," said Molly, pulling the blanket up to her chin and sinking deeper into the couch. Secretly she believed her mother might be correct. The dual existence had entered her blood stream and was poisoning her. The situation was even worse than an affair—in an affair, at least one of her lovers would know, would help her pull off the duplicity. But who was her mother to criticize? In fact, how could she even trust her mother? Her mother had been an accomplice. Molly had heard her mother lie to both Jay and Nick without even a trace of deceit in her voice. So had Abby. She did it with ease and confidence, never complaining to Molly about being asked to carry out such a massive deception. Was there anyone Molly could trust? I'm just being paranoid, she thought, because I'm sick and have a weakened resistance.

Molly fell asleep and dreamed she was pregnant and unsure whether she carried Nick's child or Jay's. In her dream, she wasn't worried about the father's identity—she felt she could keep them both believing the baby was his for two or three years, until the baby began talking, then she could get a few more months by training the baby to call Nick papa, and Jay daddy. What did concern her in the dream was the forthcoming delivery—how to have both Jay and Nick present for the birth? She couldn't think of a way to get them in and out of the delivery room in unison, nor could she imagine a doctor going along with such a farce. It was an extremely realistic dream—where she could even feel the weight of the pregnancy—filling her with so much dread that she was overcome with relief when she woke, drenched in sweat, and realized it wasn't true.

The next day when she returned to her apartment, Abby met her at the door.

"Why haven't you been answering your cell? Both Jay and Nick have been calling here—I wasn't sure what to tell them?" Molly was slightly annoyed at Abby—couldn't she handle a simple thing like what was supposed to be kept secret from whom, and making up little white lies on the spot? Molly was in the process of developing a flip retort when Abby spoke again.

"Oh, and guess what—a magazine at the beauty parlor said that bigamy is just a misdemeanor; so you can marry them both without it being much worse than a speeding ticket!"

❖

Molly had never heard what happened to Warren—or if she did, she didn't remember because in order to block her own part in the cruelty (or her failure to stop it) she needed not to know. But after the dream, he began to creep into her thoughts again. Molly wondered what it had been like for him alone in his filthy dorm room, calculating distances. She remembered the mounds of papers, drawings of triangles, each labeled with Warren's dorm window in one corner, the tree facing it in another, and varying elements in the third—the library, student union, or another place of significance to him. Molly wondered if his mother felt guilty for allowing him to go to college so early. Had he returned to college and, if so, had he amounted to anything, or had a happy life?

When she called her lovers, she learned that Jay was angry because she hadn't returned his calls, and Nick was worried that something might have happened to her. Given these two different reactions, Molly felt closer to Nick. She became frantic with the thought that he would discover her relationship with Jay, take it badly, draw into himself, and spend the rest of his life in the little apartment over the theater, edging around the perimeters of the room. She cancelled her planned trip to New York the following weekend in order to apartment hunt with Nick, not caring at all how angry it made Jay. In fact, she decided that if she found an apartment with Nick, she would break up with Jay. She suspected her attraction to him was based on the way he made her appear to the outside world, not how he made her feel inside.

Yet her day of apartment hunting with Nick was miserable. He was cranky the whole time, complaining as they climbed narrow staircases, that the places were too expensive and didn't have outdoor space for his herbs. And of course nothing was as cheap as his current place. Molly was surprised that she had never noticed how selfish he was! Immediately afterwards, she called Jay and apologized for canceling her trip.

She said she wanted to take off time from her job immediately and see what living in New York would be like, but he said no, he was coming out. He already had the ticket and would be in Chicago that very night.

"Do you want me to meet you at the airport?" she asked. She knew he liked it when she did that.

"No," he said. "I'll catch a cab. I'll be there in time for dinner, about 7:30."

To prevent any possible errors, Molly called High Vanity and told Nick she planned to go to bed early and not to come over after work. At 7:15, she began watching for the yellow cab from her window, thinking what it would be like to be married to Jay, being able to decide to fly out of town at a moment's notice. Traveling. Having a great apartment in New York. Wintering in the islands. He didn't have unlimited wealth, but more than she had ever known, and the promise of becoming wealthier with age. Nick would probably become craggier. Cooks were not known for their calm temperaments. But, on the other hand, when Nick was there, he was really present. When she rested her head on Nick's chest, his flesh contoured to the shape of her head. Jay never totally relaxed. His body was always a little tense. She couldn't just lie around with him an entire Sunday. He was better playing to a crowd. Of course, that was one of the things she liked about him—his social ease. Nick couldn't just blend in with any group. He became quiet if he didn't know people well. That was one of the things that Molly's father didn't like about Nick, his inability to make conversation. A woman had never had two clearer choices—why couldn't she make one? Molly almost wished someone would just make it for her. When she saw the yellow cab pull up to the curb, she grabbed her jacket. She didn't want to make Jay walk to the door.

When they were seated in the Red Tomato and had both ordered drinks, Molly noticed Jay's bag wasn't there.

"Oh, my God, Jay, where's your bag? Did you leave it in the cab?"

Jay looked into his drink. Bourbon and water. Jay drank like a grown-up.

"No, Molly. My bag's at the hotel."

"Hotel? Why? What's up? Why are we going to a hotel?"

She watched him turn the glass around in his hands, the bourbon catching and refracting the light, clear and amber angles. She had always liked his fingers. They were long and elegant. Nick's were big and strong, but too white and a little doughy looking.

"We're not," he said, still not looking up. "That's why I came out, Molly. I need to tell you, Molly, face-to-face, that we've got to end this. It's ridiculous."

Molly could barely believe her ears.

"What are you talking about?"

"Us. I've known for a long time that things weren't going right, but I thought, well, if you moved—but that bit with the apartment—ghosts!—we looked like asses in front of that agent."

Still looking into his drink, he shook his head back and forth slowly.

"Nick," she said, a hysterical giggle escaping her throat. It was the first time she had made that mistake. Jay didn't even notice. Nick would have. "Jay, I'm sorry. You're right. I was wrong. But I'm sure we can do something to fix it."

"No, Molly, not this time."

He looked up. She could tell from the cold look in his eyes— she had seen it before at work—that his mind was decided. How could it be that the last time she had seen this face, she had had control over it? Could make it smile, pout, or laugh? And now she could do nothing?

Fighting back tears, she ate half her plate of gnocchi, each bite a dry lump barely able travel down her throat. She thought if she didn't leave right away, if she tried to appear unruffled and finish, her sense of inner calm would surface. She would get the same

174

feeling she had at the robbery and be able to come up with a laundry list of explanations why they shouldn't break-up, why her behavior at the loft was excusable. But nothing came to her.

"I'm going to get a cab," she said.

"Why don't you wait until I'm finished, then I'll see you home."

"No." Molly stood and pushed in her seat. With effort, she managed to control herself until she walked outside and found a cab. Her throat hurt, as if half of the gnocchi was paused midway down it. She had planned on giving the cabbie her address, instead she heard herself providing directions to High Vanity.

"Wait, I'll just be a minute," Molly told the driver as he sidled the curb. Before he could respond, she dashed from the door. Since she had not paid him, he had no choice but to wait. High Vanity wasn't crowded so Ralph saw her before she even got to the bar.

"Do you want me to get Nick?" he asked.

"No, I just need to write him a note," said Molly. She pulled a paper cocktail napkin from the stack on the bar, a pen from her purse, and wrote across the surface, her block letters pressing into the soft paper like a stick into wet cement:

I AM VERY SORRY BUT I CAN'T SEE YOU ANY MORE. MY FAULT, NOT YOURS. DON'T CALL.

LOVE, M.

She folded the napkin, creased it, and slid it across the bar to Ralph.

"Please wait until the end of his shift before you give it to him."

"Molly," said Ralph, a vague pleading concern in his tone. Her face must have been blotched from crying. "Why don't I go get Nick?"

When had everyone started talking to her as if she was crazy?

"No, Ralph, and don't give it to him until the end of his shift —or you might have a chef walking out before the late crowd. I've got to go. The meter is running."

Back in the cab, she gave her mother's address. By the time she arrived, the fare was almost sixty dollars. She told the driver to wait while she went inside and got her money. Her mother was asleep.

"Mom, mom," she whispered into the dark of her mother's bedroom. "I need some money. The cab driver's waiting outside for sixty dollars, and I've only got thirty."

"Oh, Molly, Molly, Molly," her mother mumbled into her pillow. "I was hoping to go to sleep early tonight. My purse is on the dresser."

§

The sum of all the angles of a triangles is 180 degrees, which, when doubled, becomes 360 degrees—in other words, a circle. Molly sat at the small desk by the window where she used to do her homework, and looked out on the backyard. She pictured the way the point the compass used to perforate her notebook paper as she drove the spike holding the little saffron colored pencil around. That's how Molly felt her life had gone since she graduated from college and met Nick: in a complete circle. From being alone to having two men to being alone. From her mother's house to college to an apartment with a friend, then back to her mother's house. She remembered her right hand twisting the compass around until she was forced to transfer it to her left.

In the center of the backyard was what her mother called a Tree of Heaven because of the speed with which the tree grew —"as if reaching for heaven." It was a huge leafy tree beneath which Molly set up doll tea parties when she was young. Once when her father arrived early to get her, as she collected her tea things, he had walked around the yard like a king surveying his former kingdom, his hands crammed in his pockets, as if to prevent himself from reclaiming anything. "Well, at least I don't have to deal with the Weed Tree now," he had said. Later Molly had asked her mother why he called it that.

"You know all those little trees—or big weeds—we pull up all summer, the ones with the deep roots? They're seeds from the tree that grow like 'weeds,' her mother had sighed. "Heaven. Weeds. I guess, is the basic difference between your father and me."

Molly quit her job over the phone, stayed at her mother's house for three weeks, and rarely left her room. Nick had called daily in the beginning, but Molly's mother had convinced him that Molly wouldn't talk. It was lucky, Molly thought, as she gazed out the window, that she wasn't as skilled at Math as Warren or she might be using her girlhood window and the tree as starting points for multiple drawings of triangulation. In another week, Molly would be moving to California. She had told her mother she needed to go far away. She had saved a little

177

money, but not enough for California. Her mother had given Molly some money, and had gotten Molly's father to contribute by pretending Molly had had a nervous breakdown. Now, as she looked across the yard, Molly wondered if her mother had pretended to her father or had pretended to her that she was only pretending with him?

◈

During the first year in Los Angeles, after she found a job, Molly liked to ride the train down to San Diego for the weekend. If she got her seat early, she could get a window on a seat facing south going down, and north going up, enabling her to watch the ocean both ways. On her third trip back from San Diego, she found a perfect seat by a window. Seated in front of her were two young men, Mexican or South American. As Molly waited for the train to start—it was already a few minutes behind the scheduled departure—she listened desultorily to the men chatter in Spanish. They stopped speaking when a stocky man and a tall woman entered the car with a purposeful walk. Hips swinging forward than back, the two strode directly to the seat of the men in front of Molly. The woman was skinny with thin blond hair just reaching her shoulders—as if she had pulled it there and sprayed it in place—and the man was built as if he worked out a lot at Muscle Beach. Both wore sunglasses. The woman addressed the two men.

"Where were you born?"

The men looked at each other as if they didn't understand. Molly didn't understand either. What kind of questions was that? Where were you born? Not only a non-sequitur, but a rude one.

Then it hit Molly—the man and woman were border patrol, the men were illegal aliens. Still it seemed a strange way to begin an interrogation

"I asked, where were you born?" The woman repeated, more harshly this time.

Illinois, Molly wanted to whisper. Her lips were just inches from their glowing pink ears, suffused with the glare of the sun coming in the window. She could see a thin scarlet vein curving through the right ear of the man closest to the window. Chicago, Molly whispered, too softly for anyone but herself to hear. The blonde woman put her hands on her hips, which pushed back the bottom of her thin nylon jacket, exposing a gun and a badge clipped to her belt. Molly stared at the gun, remembering how it had all started with Nick. The metal against her forehead. She felt a surge of readiness, underpinned by calm; if called upon she felt she could provide the men with a list of explanations for why they should be permitted to continue on their journeys. She knew she would not be asked, but that wasn't the point. She could handle the situation by herself if the need arose.

The woman yanked the man closest to her up from the seat. Her muscled companion reached in for the other man. Looking around blankly, the young men did not resist as they were cuffed together. Both were dressed in new dark blue jeans and neatly pressed plaid shirts, tucked into their pants. Groomed for their new lives. A lump rose in Molly's throat as she watched them being led down the aisle, then watched out the window as the foursome emerged from the train. The woman—still holding her charge by his upper arm—spoke into a walkie-talkie. A second later, Molly felt the tug of the train leaving the station. Pressing her brow against the glass, she twisted her neck to watch as the two men were led to a van. It seemed a robbery of sorts. But she couldn't quite figure out who was robbing whom? As the train pulled from the station, Molly strained to see them, thinking how quickly the lines between her and them were lengthening, how in a few days these men—who she could have reached out and touched only a minute before—would be, like so many others, far, far behind her.

THE WEDDING INVITATION

The envelope sat atop the pile of mail on the dining room table when Priscilla got home. Lush, cream-colored paper. Their names stacked above their address like tiers on a wedding cake:

Tom Hill

Dr. Priscilla Ann Bentley

20355 South West Cranberry Avenue

Priscilla slit the envelope with the pewter letter opener she kept between the candlesticks. The invitation was expensive, engraved in Park Avenue script, with a stamped reply envelope.

She didn't recognize the names of the betrothed—Ellen Merryweather and Lewis Anderson. Probably friends of Tom's, Priscilla thought; his friends were still at the stage in their lives where they threw big weddings. She quickly sorted the rest of the pile, and went into the bathroom to freshen her make-up.

At forty, Priscilla was ten years older than Tom. Seven years ago, he had been a student in her graduate workshop. Priscilla had resisted the relationship.

A tawdry affair with a student could have destroyed everything. She was a rising star. An up-and-coming poet. Her third book had just received the prestigious Homer Award. Besides, Priscilla couldn't bear to think that she had anything in common with those pathetic men in her department who sometimes dated students. She considered them insecure, unable to compete in an arena of more mature women.

But Tom kept appearing. At her readings, her office, and finally, even at her apartment. He always stood inappropriately close, so that she could feel the heat of his body, his breath on her face, the tension thickening with each moment, with each question he asked. Do you think this line breaks at the right place? What about this image? Does that part sound contrived? And she would always accommodate him. As if it were perfectly natural for an award-winning poet to drop everything to ponder the word choice of a student who hadn't even made an appointment.

The first time she had invited him into her home, it had been to avoid the appearance of impropriety. She didn't want to be seen talking to him on the bright street in front of the large old Victorian house where she rented an apartment.

His kiss had taken her by surprise. She had turned from the sink to hand him a glass of water. He had taken the glass—a heavy rock glass she had purchased in a set of six—and moved to reach around her and place it on the counter, his face meeting hers midway in the maneuver.

His mouth tasted wet and deep. And, she had to admit, young. Eager. She might have been able to pull away if he hadn't pressed his palm to her breastplate, above and between her breasts, a move that electrified her nipples, making it impossible to stop what was started.

❦

"Who is Ellen Merryweather?" she asked at dinner, removing the salad bowls so she could serve the soup. She assumed most couples became more casual at dinner as their marriage matured, sometimes having just a sandwich or calling out for pizza. With Priscilla and Tom, the opposite had happened. Each year brought another course or tradition, new formalities.

"I give up. Who is she?" asked Tom, displaying his impish grin. Priscilla felt herself softening. The "I give up" line was a private joke, one that always got a laugh. Tom had used it the first time she asked him a question in class. The playful impertinence had disarmed her, cracked her up, a vast departure from her usual classroom demeanor.

"On the wedding invitation we received. Ellen Merryweather and, let me see . . ." she put the salad plates back down, and went to the sideboard where she had placed the mail. "Lewis Anderson."

"Never heard of either of them," said Tom, flipping back the linen napkin covering the basket of rolls to seize one. It was ridiculous, Priscilla knew, but she resented the way he snatched it, as if the rolls were just there, for his taking! He acted as if no time had gone into preparing them, keeping them warm, and putting them on the table. In the beginning of their relationship, he had been almost as fascinated by her culinary skills as he had been by her accomplishments as a poet.

"Me neither," she said. "But it's addressed to both of us."

"Mr. and Mrs. Tom Hill or our separate names?"

"Our separate names."

"It's probably a student of yours," said Tom.

Using her hip to open the swinging door, Priscilla went into the kitchen to ladle up the soup into pretty Wedgwood bowls. She and Tom had purchased their Wedgwood at an estate sale.

Place settings for twenty. As they had loaded the boxes into the car, they had laughed at the idea that they might ever have a dinner for twenty. But Tom loved the china. He was from a lower middle class family and marveled at the fact that Priscilla knew things about china, fabric, furniture, fine foods, and etiquette. In fact, she didn't know near as much as it appeared. It was just that she felt a growing obligation to learn—and to show Tom that there wasn't anything she couldn't teach him.

"I doubt it," she said, re-entering the room, clutching both bowls by their rims. "I'd remember any student I knew well enough to be invited to her wedding."

Tom swallowed the first spoonful of his soup without a word. Then a second. He dipped in for a third.

"Do you like it?" asked Priscilla.

"Oh, I'm sorry," said Tom. "It's great—I just drifted off; I was daydreaming."

Priscilla had spent her office hours flipping through cookbooks, looking for a warm-weather soup that she hadn't tried yet. They were experiencing a particularly hot spring. This recipe had required almost an hour of additional work— running to the store for ingredients, finely chopping cucumbers and scallions. Subtle spices. Anyone else would have been impressed. She thought of Neil Duffy, the Joyce scholar in the department— what he would have given to be in Tom's place! During her first year in the department, Neil had wanted to ask her out, had given her obvious feelers in order to be sure of his ground before actually asking, risking having to spend years working with a woman who had rejected him. Priscilla had made it clear how she would respond. But she couldn't help thinking now, as she stared at her daydreaming husband, that Neil never would have shown her so little regard.

"Daydreaming about what? That bitch, Ellen Merryweather?" she asked, her voice suddenly spitting, contemptuous.

Tom froze, his spoon poised ridiculously mid-air, in front of his lips, his eyes wide with alarm. He lowered the spoon back into the bowl.

"What do you mean by that?"

Priscilla giggled, embarrassed.

"I was only joking," she said.

❖

Their affair had been risky. They had to keep it a secret until Tom graduated. But every time they were in a class together, regardless of how far apart they sat from one another, Priscilla felt a beacon of hot light connecting them. If she felt it, surely, she thought, everyone else must. She tried not to look at him, to maintain the same tone of voice she used with other students. Yet how could she use an urgent whisper, ripe with desire, at night and switch to a formal, authoritative voice in the light of day?

She had never felt so weak, so self-destructive. If he came to her office, she always said, "No, not here." But even she didn't believe her words. She grew light as air when he strode behind her desk, lifted her by the armpits, and pressed her to the wall. Once, they had made love between the window and the bookcase, her body parts melting, turning to liquid, while two students waited outside her door.

Not telling anyone was the easiest part. Priscilla had never been particularly social. As a girl, she had been a bookworm. Though considered quite attractive, she had only had one serious relationship in college. As a woman, she had rejected more men than she had dated. Until she met Tom, she believed there would be plenty of time for romance later. She was in love with her poetry. All of her time outside of school was spent writing, submitting her work, and reading other poets. Tom made her realize time was running out.

They were married the spring Tom graduated, a month after Priscilla received her formal letter securing tenure. The wedding was small. A few of her students, the other poet from the department, her best friend from college, and the woman who had been her next door neighbor when she still lived in the apartment in the Victorian house. A few of Tom's friends. And Priscilla's father, the only parent out of four who didn't disapprove of the match.

Within months of the wedding, Tom put on a little weight, grew a beard. It was almost as if he were quickening the appearance of aging out of consideration for Priscilla. Everyone remarked on it. A few even made it sound as if Priscilla should be pleased by this transformation. As if she had not knowingly married a man ten years her junior. But his aging bothered her. She knew it was false. Temporary. With a week of exercise and a few swipes of the razor, he could get rid of it all. Hers was real. Besides, she didn't want him to look older. If she had wanted an older man she could have taken up with Neil Duffy. "Have you thought of taking up a pipe?" she had asked during one of her rare bitter days in the beginning.

"Why would I do that?" he asked, honestly bewildered. She had laughed, relieved he hadn't caught her sarcasm, and passed it off as silliness.

❖

The wedding invitation nagged at Priscilla the next day. It distracted her through both her undergraduate workshop and the monthly full-time faculty meeting.

The discussion at the meeting centered on the rights of parttime and adjunct faculty. Oscar Newton, a gangly Victorian literature scholar whose shoulders were always covered with dandruff, delivered a prolix speech on the virtues of maintaining strict boundaries between full and part-time faculty. He said that to "grant part-time faculty any more privileges would be to foster a sense of false hope that a tenure-track position might become available for them." Neil Duffy concurred. Absorbed with speculation about the strange woman who had sent them a wedding invitation, Priscilla barely listened. But when Oscar rambled on about part-time faculty having too much access to the photocopy machine, Priscilla exploded.

"Oh, that's a bunch of rubbish, Oscar, and you know it. The part-time faculty around here are paid slave wages; we could at least treat them with a little respect. Not make them beg for every copy they make."

The room fell suddenly silent. Then Priscilla reddened at the realization that Tom was part-time faculty, and everyone in the room knew it.

After the meeting, Priscilla went back to the office and pulled her records. She kept grade sheets dating back five years. She went through each file carefully, checking off individual names with a pencil. No Ellen Merryweather or Lewis Anderson. Surely no student who predated five years would invite her to a wedding? And how would such a student even be aware of Tom's name?

Priscilla suspected that Ellen was a former girlfriend and Tom was trying to spare her feelings. Priscilla decided to confront him that evening, let him know she wasn't jealous or possessive. They both had former lives. It was best to be honest with each other. Besides, Priscilla thought, but wouldn't tell him, what did she have to fear of Ellen Merryweather? She was getting married.

❖

During their courtship, Priscilla had been careful not to mention their age difference. Every time she expressed doubts about their union, she attributed her concerns to her bid for tenure or the ethics of a student/teacher relationship. She didn't want to plant ideas in Tom's head. She knew that if she referred to herself as old, eventually he would begin to see her that way.

The first time their age difference was even spoken aloud was a year after they were married and Tom took Priscilla back to Missouri to meet his parents. They lived in a ranch house on a street where some of the houses were well maintained; others had cars sitting on blocks in the front yard. Tom's parents' house was one of the nicer ones. The grass was cut and green. Along the concrete driveway, the weeds had been trimmed with a Weed

Whacker. In the center of the yard an enormous tire, spray painted white, was used as a planter for bright red geraniums.

All the furniture in his parents' narrow living room was pressed up against the walls. Two chairs and an end table sat beneath the picture window. A long aqua couch with blond wood arms—beneath an even longer mirror, appliqued with gold swans—was shoved up against the other wall. At one end of the room was the doorway to the hall. At the other end, a monstrous color television squatted.

Priscilla and Tom sat on the couch, his parents facing them in the two chairs. They drank weak coffee from cheap transparent glass mugs that Tom's mother obviously thought were stylish. Tom's mother was only eighteen when Tom was born, which meant she was closer in age to Priscilla than Tom was. But Mrs. Hill was already a grandmother. Both her younger daughters had babies. Tom was the only one to go to college.

"We wanted Tom to be a doctor or a lawyer or something. He's smart enough," said the father. "But he got hooked on this poetry stuff."

He said poetry the same way he might have said "drugs."

"We just don't get it," his mother said, and then looked at Priscilla. Slightly slack jawed, she was twenty pounds overweight with hair bleached a Marilyn Monroe white-blond. Though neither parent looked like Tom, his mother's eyes might have resembled Tom's if they hadn't been encased in charcoal black eyeliner. "You've been at it a while. Is there any money in it? Any future?"

Tom had a little smile on his face, waiting to see how Priscilla would react. In another situation, Priscilla might have scoffed.

Or laughed. Money in poetry! But out of respect for Tom, she tried to answer seriously.

"You rarely make much of a profit from your books, but you can teach. I make a nice living from it."

Tom's father shook his head sadly. But the mother's disapproval was even more apparent. All through the conversation, she asked questions aimed at exposing Priscilla as too old and worldly for her son. Have you ever been divorced? How old are your parents? Do you dye your hair? She had a method of embedding the particularly offensive questions in statements that made them appear innocuous. For instance, she asked about Priscilla's hair in the context of statements about her own hair coloring problems. Priscilla's parents came up when she mentioned the nursing home where she worked as an aide. And the divorce question was carefully woven into a story about her cousin's divorce. Normally Priscilla would have found a polite way to refuse to answer. But she sensed that Tom's mother, Cindy, was a high-strung woman who would—with the slightest provocation—snap at Priscilla.

Later at dinner, Priscilla's instincts proved correct. They went to a restaurant that Cindy called "fancy," though there were no cloths on the tables and the only kinds of wine they served were "red" and "white," no other distinctions. Still, Cindy had too much to drink and became sloppy and mean. She called Priscilla "snooty" when Priscilla asked if they had sauvignon blanc. They said white or red! And she told Tom he should see a "shrink for marrying a woman old enough to be his mother." "Calm down, mom," Tom had whispered across the tabletop of the restaurant booth. "Pris would have had to have had a baby at ten to be my mom."

His mother simply hiccupped and drained her glass of pale pink wine.

"My son, the poet, going to see the shrink to find out why he married his mother, the professor," Cindy said, slapping the table. "I never thought I'd see the day!"

"Cindy," began Priscilla in a careful soothing tone. "We're not . . ."

"Cindy, Cindy, Cindy," said Cindy in a high-pitched mocking voice. "How about Mrs. Hill? Or why don't you call me 'mom' like my sons-in-law's do? Do you feel foolish calling someone so close to your own age mom?"

"Okay, Cindy, I think we better get you home," said Tom's father, trying to lift his wife up by the armpits the same way Tom had that time in Priscilla's office. But Cindy wouldn't budge. Instead she leaned across the table, her mascara so badly smeared that she resembled an albino raccoon. She pointed a finger at Priscilla.

"You can win for now," she slurred. "But in the long run, I'll be the winner. I'll always be his mother. But you won't always be his wife. He'll never have kids with you. In fact, you'll never be anyone's mother."

Priscilla knew it was the rantings of a drunken woman. Still she was stung hard, as if Cindy were a Cassandra, marking Priscilla's future with her words.

The next morning at breakfast in Tom's parents' kitchen, they were all polite and quiet. On the plane ride home, Tom attempted to apologize, but Priscilla hushed him.

"Don't worry. It's not your fault," she said. "I don't even blame her. I realize she hasn't had the advantages of money or an education."

As if, Priscilla thought as she said calmed Tom, an educated woman would not have noticed the ten-year age difference.

❖

When Priscilla arrived home, she was surprised to see the mail still jammed in the flat black box next to the front door. After her outburst at the faculty meeting, she was feeling cranky. She balanced the bag of groceries on her hip in order to free her right hand to unwedge the mail. She took the stack inside and slapped it down on the dining room table next to a note from Tom:

> Pris— I went to a ball game. Don't wait dinner.
> I'll be home late. Love, Tom

A ball game? Tom had never done such a thing without mentioning it days in advance. She glanced at the bag on her hip. So, she wondered, what am I supposed to do with these? A dozen different types of fresh vegetables to prepare ratatouille. She decided to go ahead and make it. She could always reheat it the next night.

Priscilla pretended to herself that she enjoyed her time alone in the kitchen—the way she used to before she knew Tom— chopping up vegetables, thickening the sauce, while listening to a Billie Holiday CD. It got so hot that she pinned her hair up.

Damp tendrils broke free. She recalled kissing Tom's neck last summer, right after they had bought the house, when he was sweaty from working in the yard. She had liked the salty taste, the texture of his firm skin.

This is nice, she thought, trying to convince herself, working in the kitchen while my husband is at a ball game. I will eat just a small portion, store the rest, and then go work on that poem I wrote last week. I rarely have the house to myself anymore!

Usually Priscilla enjoyed revising her poetry. The process reminded her of running a brush through her hair, over and over, until all the foreign particles had been removed and it shone. But that night she couldn't make any progress. She kept getting stuck. Nothing worked. With each change, the poem sounded more trite.

She tried to read a book, mend a blouse, watch television, but these activities seemed absurd on such a lovely spring evening. She considered taking a walk, but didn't want to be outside by herself once darkness descended.

So she sat on the sofa and watched the light grow faint. Is this what it would be like to be a woman living by myself, she wondered, terrified? Before Tom, she had been a woman on the brink. But now, she would be a middle-aged woman with few friends. She studied her hands, the way the skin was beginning to leather. She curled in a ball and looked at her feet. Her toenails, she noticed, were becoming more calcified, slightly yellow. The room turned a monochromatic dark gray, yet she didn't move to switch on a light. Instead, she thought of Tom, out with Ellen Merryweather. Priscilla could envisage how it happened. Ellen suggested they have a drink to toast her marriage. But in the bar, sharing old memories from their undergraduate days, they would realize they were still in love. Tom would convince Ellen not to go through with her plans, promise to leave his wife.

Or perhaps Ellen Merryweather was a student of Tom's. Just because his students were freshman didn't mean they couldn't get married. Look at Tom's own mother; she had been a teenage bride. Or maybe, Priscilla shuddered, Ellen wasn't getting married at all. She had simply had one invitation printed and sent to Tom, a ploy to make him jealous and convince him to leave Priscilla.

By the time she heard Tom's key in the lock a little before midnight, Priscilla had been sitting on the couch in the dark for hours.

"Pris," he said when he saw her. "What are you doing in the dark?"

"Where have you been?" she demanded.

"Didn't you see my note?" he asked, coming to sit next to her on the sofa. He smelled of beer.

"What type of ball game lasts until midnight?"

"It went into an extra inning, then we went out for a few beers."

"Who is we?" she asked, her eyes narrowing into slits. "You and Ellen Merryweather?"

"Who?"

"Oh, like you don't know! That slut on the wedding invitation!" The bile in Priscilla's voice surprised even her.

"I don't believe this," said Tom. "I have no idea who that woman is."

"Yeah, right, just like you couldn't call to tell me you were going out. You had to leave a note."

"I tried to call. You weren't in your office, so I just left a note. Rick Watson didn't know he had an extra ticket until the last minute."

"Uh-huh," she said. "And you have to do whatever Rick Watson wants you to do."

Suddenly Tom was angry, angrier than Priscilla had ever seen him. He leapt from the couch yelling. "This is a bunch of shit! I didn't do anything wrong. I shouldn't have to call my mommy to get permission to go to a stupid ball game."

For just a second, Tom looked like his mother had that night years ago, in the restaurant, slack-jawed and mean.

Priscilla burst into tears.

Tom sat down beside her, himself again, stroking her hair, hugging her.

"I'm sorry, Pris, I'm really sorry. I didn't mean to hurt you. I really didn't. I didn't say 'mommy' because you're older; I said it because I felt like I couldn't do what I wanted."

It was too late; the words they had been so careful not to utter for years had been spoken.

That night, Tom was gentle in their lovemaking, but Priscilla sensed it was more to keep her at bay, to placate her, than to bring her closer. In the morning, she wasn't the least bit surprised when he went into the bathroom without a word, and emerged with a clean-shaven face.

So far, Cindy's words had proven prophetic. Priscilla had not become pregnant. The first two years they had been waiting until Tom got a book published. The third year of their marriage he had spent looking for a job. One modestly reviewed book from a small press was only enough to get him two interviews at colleges in the Midwest. Priscilla couldn't relinquish a tenured job. And the only offer he did receive wasn't enough money to make commuting feasible. So they agreed it was easier for him to teach freshman composition part-time in Priscilla's department. He could be their baby's primary caretaker.

But Priscilla didn't get pregnant.

Despite physicals that gave them both clean slates, Priscilla could not conceive. They discussed seeing fertility doctors, but time kept slipping by without either of them making that move.

❖

"You know," said Tom, as they were both getting ready for the writing program's end of the year poetry reading. "I hate to bring this up, but we need to send a reply for that wedding."

Priscilla froze, her head tilted to receive a pearl earring. Since the night of the ball game, a distance had grown between them. Their roles had experienced a subtle reversal. Tom seemed more mature. At times an indulgent parent—or simply a tolerant one. "Why? Do you want to go?"

"No, of course not. I told you, I don't even know the people. I do not know Ellen Merryweather. I do not know Ellen

Merryweather. I do not know Ellen Merryweather. Enough?" Tom said impatiently, knotting his tie, pulling it through the loop to slap against his hard stomach. He had lost weight. "But they are planning an expensive wedding—you could tell by the invitation—it's rude not to R.S.V.P."

Who was he to tell her such a thing? A year ago, he wouldn't have even thought about an R.S.V.P.

"All right, then. You mail it. Tell them no," she said, hating the petulance in her voice, but incapable of anything else. "I want nothing to do with it."

The reading garnered a large audience. Preceding Priscilla were five student poets, the other department poet, an assistant professor, and a visiting poet. As most distinguished, Priscilla came last. The readers sat in the front row of the auditorium. Priscilla looked around several times, but couldn't spot Tom. They had become separated soon after their arrival. She noticed Neil Duffy sat in the third row with a woman, who appeared to be under forty—but of course Priscilla couldn't see whether she had crow's feet or a disintegrating jaw line, the telltale signs, from such a distance.

When Priscilla finally climbed the steps to the stage, her ascension was met with loud applause. She was not nervous. She had given countless readings. Moving behind the podium, waiting for the clapping to subside, her eyes raked the audience. There was Tom, in the far-left corner, engaged in conversation with a young woman beside him. No wonder she hadn't spotted him earlier. With his hairless face, he looked years younger.

"For my first poem . . ." Priscilla began, her voice cracking. Tom broke off discussion with the woman next to him to face the stage. "For my first poem, I'd like to read from a series I wrote last summer. It is . . ."

To her surprise, her voice remained unsteady throughout the entire reading. When she finished, the applause was less certain than that of her greeting. She was too distracted to respond to any of their questions appropriately. When she descended the steps, fewer people than usual came up to compliment her. Tom was nowhere to be seen. Usually he was the first to the stage, standing beside her, proudly enjoying her praise.

"What poets most influenced you?" asked the father of a student.

"Excuse me," she said, as she brushed past the man without answering. "I need to go find my husband."

Priscilla pushed through the crowd, blindly bumping into people, shoving them aside, her anxiety level rising with each passing moment. When she spotted him in the lobby, talking with the same young woman with whom he had been sitting, Priscilla felt her heart plunge through her ribcage. Stricken in her tracks. Ellen Merryweather? Working to regain her composure, she strode to Tom's side, linking her arm through his.

"Hi, Pris," he said, kissing her cheek. "I've got some interesting news. But first I'd like you to meet Vicky Adams. She's another part-timer."

The young woman stuck out her hand and Priscilla shook it. Vicky was thin and athletic with shiny, short dark hair.

"Nice reading," said Vicky. "I really loved the last poem."

"Oh, yeah, honey, I'm sorry—you were great," said Tom. "But Vicky just told me some interesting news. The visiting poet at Worden had a family emergency, and had to cancel for this year.

198

I guess they're really stuck since there is so little time to advertise before fall. Vicky knows the program director. She thinks I'll have a really good shot if I call Monday."

"That's great," said Priscilla, an artificial smile plastered on her face. "But I thought we agreed commuting across country isn't worth it."

"Yeah, but this is only a one year appointment. It's not the same as taking a permanent position. Even if I could only come back once during the whole year, it would be worth it to get a full-time poetry gig on my C.V."

"So, tell me, Vicky," asked Priscilla, still smiling. "Why aren't you following up on this wonderful opportunity?"

"Oh, I don't have a book or anything yet," said Vicky. "Besides, my daughter is so young that she needs both of her parents at home right now."

Knowing she had no case—she had exhausted all her unreasonable behavior with the Ellen Merryweather affair—Priscilla just continued to stand there, beaming, gripping Tom's arm.

❖

Priscilla stood in front of the frozen food case, selecting individual-sized diet dinners. With Tom away, she had taken to only making a salad each night to accompany a microwaved dish.

It was the week before Thanksgiving. Originally they had planned for Tom to come home for the holiday. But two weeks ago he had called to say that fares were ridiculously high for a four-day trip. Besides, Thanksgiving was a crowded time to travel. Unpleasant. It would be better if he just took the entire two weeks at Christmas. There was a distant formality to his voice that discouraged Priscilla from arguing.

As she arranged the frozen boxes in the cart, Priscilla saw her former neighbor, Pat Harris, approaching. A few years older than Priscilla, Pat and her teenage son had lived in an apartment in the old Victorian house where Priscilla used to rent. She had always liked Pat, one of the few guests at her own wedding.

"Priscilla, where have you been hiding?" asked Pat. "I haven't seen you since last winter. I know you're always buried in work —but you used to break away for lunch or a drink every now and then. "

"Tom has taken a year appointment out of town this year, so we wanted to spend as much time alone together as possible before he left. We've never been separated before."

"Oh, is that why you missed the wedding?"

"Wedding?" asked Priscilla. Her scalp prickled with fear and growing comprehension.

"In June. Lew, my son's wedding. I know you got the invitation. We received the R.S.V.P."

"Pat," Priscilla sighed, truly sorry, more sorry than she could ever express. "I apologize. I didn't know that was your son. I didn't recognize the name." Pat groaned.

"Oh, no wonder, I told them this might happen. Lew has my ex-husband's last name. I wanted to put the parent's names on the invitation, but the kids insisted otherwise. Ellen's parents are divorced as well, and she thought it would look funny, be a bad omen or something, to have four single parents with different last names," said Pat. "I'm sorry."

"No, it's not your fault," said Priscilla. "It's mine."

When Pat and Priscilla parted, agreeing to call each other soon to make lunch plans, Priscilla felt old and tired. Her legs stiff. If things were different, she would call Tom and tell him. They could have a great laugh over the misunderstanding. But she didn't want to bring up any subject that might trigger an early cancellation of their Christmas plans. She knew the cancellation was coming, but she wanted to postpone it, delay the heart ache she expected—all that she had known was inevitable—from the moment years ago in the kitchen when she didn't move as he reached around her to place the heavy glass on the counter.

These days, now that they no longer need to save for the future, Stanley and Carol stay in luxury hotels. Rooms with thick terry cloth robes hanging in the closets. Suites with wet bars. Mints on the pillows at night. Beds so tightly made that Carol feels she is slipping into a giant's starched white shirt pocket. Yet they like to visit the kinds of places where they used to stay when they were younger: motels, ramshackle inns, even flophouses. It is as if viewing such places allowed them a glimpse into their past. A time when poverty was an adventure. A time when a room became theirs simply because they shared it for a night.

A time when all promises were good.

Though they never plan these trips to hotels where they don't intend to stay, the excursions happen almost every time they travel. Most visits go the same way. Certain vacancy signs simply draw them in. Stanley pretends to the desk clerk that they are interested in registering. Drumming his fingers on the desk, looking this way and that, he casually asks, "May we take a peek at a room? We're thinking of staying the night." Carol can't remember a clerk refusing them.

That was how it had started with this place. They were driving down the Canadian coast on the way to visit Russell, their eldest son, and came upon the large frame structure on the edge of a fishing town. Following the sweeping curve of the bay, they spotted the ocean side first. The hotel loomed across the water. Sided in gray shingles, the huge building almost seemed to be leaning toward the waves. A dangerous curtsey. Shutters and flower boxes, a few narrow balconies, all overlooked the water.

Only a thin strip of land separated the hotel from the badly eroded bluff.

As Stanley pulled up to the place, they saw that the rear faced the road: garbage pails clouded with flies and a steep wall criss-crossed with a rickety wooden fire escape. The shingles were mottled and faded, like flowered cloth that had been bleached, then hung out in the sun for many summer days on end.

"All the available rooms are open," said the clerk without looking up from the yellowing fishing magazine he flipped through. Carol tried to see the illustrations, but her vision was no longer good enough to reconstruct upside-down images. She knew her impression—men kissing big fish—couldn't be correct.

Nearly vertical, the old staircase was so narrow that they were forced to climb single file. The climb didn't bother them. They were in good shape for their age. Carol gardened and swam. And despite slightly elevated blood pressure, Stanley still managed to play tennis twice a week. They weren't even breathing heavily by the time they reached the second floor.

Most of the doors stood open. They examined every room. Beds and upholstered furniture sagged. Curtains and bedspreads were thin, tattered, or mended. Yet the color schemes were so exaggerated that both Stanley and Carol couldn't help but be charmed. There was so much pink and red in "The Rose Room" that Carol almost felt she had entered a beating heart. The yellow room glowed, reminding Carol of Monet's dining room, without the same attention to aesthetics, in his French country home. (In recent years, they had twice visited his house and gardens.) The green room was as lush as a jungle. Someone had gone to great pains—with little regard for taste—to make sure everything matched.

Each floor contained a central hall with four rooms branching out.

Carol and Stanley climbed until they reached the top floor, the fifth, and found all the doors closed except the one labeled "The Widow's Walk," in shaky blue paint across the lintel.

The room hit Carol like a sudden breeze when she entered.

Painted cornflower blue, the interior contained two blue chairs, a double bed covered with a powder blue spread, sheer blue curtains, and a furry blue rug in the center of a wood floor with planks painted various shades of blue. The dresser was painted blue and held a blue china vase of plastic blue flowers. French doors opened onto a narrow balcony over the wide cobalt sea that appeared, through optical illusion, to rise like a wall of water. The room, itself, seemed to float high in the heavens.

Stanley also gasped at the sight. Yet Carol couldn't have been more surprised when they returned to the front desk and Stanley said, "We'll take 'The Widow's Walk.'"

The clerk, still leaning over the same magazine, reached behind him to remove a heavy key from a wall peg. He handed it to Stanley.

"That'll be thirty-nine dollars for the one night."

"Lovely decorating," said Carol, half in truth, half in irony.

"That'll be my mother you can thank for that," said the clerk.

"Though who can see the point; nobody but the fishermen that sees it most a' the time."

"We're going to go get some supper," said Stanley as he handed the clerk two twenties.

The clerk took the money, handed Stanley a single, faded by what seemed like a thousand salt-water washings, and resumed his reading.

Outside Carol giggled and looped her arm through Stanley's.

"What about Russell? He's expecting us in two hours!" whispered Carol, as if someone could hear—or would care if they did.

Seeming to stand taller, chest out, Stanley shrugged.

"What about him? He's gotten along a good twenty years without his parents. I think if we call him and tell him he can make it another night."

Again Carol giggled. She couldn't remember when last she had felt so naughty.

✧

Everything in the town needed a coat of paint and seemed to be leaning with age. Aside from a hot dog stand and a greasy diner, there was only one restaurant: an Italian place with eight tables covered in red and white plastic checkered table cloths. But the fish and pasta were fresh and the cheap red wine tasted of their youth, so they were happy. Carol twirled the stem of her glass between her fingers, watching the blue veins that had started, years ago, to loop and bulge across her hands. Half way through the bottle, their conversation turned to hotel rooms they had shared. Particularly the shabby ones during the early years of their marriage.

On their first road trip west, they had had a room so small that when Stanley used the corner walk-in shower, water sprayed

Carol in bed. During a steamy hot weekend in New Orleans they had filled the claw-footed tub of the hotel bath with buckets of ice from the machine and soaked until their young bodies turned numb.

"Remember when Russell and Peter were little and we used to hang sheets between our beds for privacy," said Carol.

"You were still afraid they would walk in on us. I think that enhanced the excitement."

Carol felt the flush of wine in her cheeks. When they had these sorts of intimate conversations, Stanley always looked boyish to her, his prominent ears becoming even more silly.

"My favorite place was our first time in Mexico, you know the place, what was it? The one right after you did the McKinney deal and we used all the money to take our first trip without the boys. On the cliff over the water. Remember, there were dozens of iguana, running all over the place like squirrels. And the water—remember how blue it looked from the cliff? Almost as blue as this place."

"What was its name?" Stanley asked, twisting his mouth in a way that reminded her of how he looked when he concentrated on something—making a kite or assembling a model—with the boys when they were young. She loved to spy on them then, from around a door or the top of the stairs, when he thought he was alone with the boys.

"Hacienda something, del Playa, del Sol, what was it?"

They had almost finished the bottle. She could tell that, like her, Stanley was slightly drunk.

"No I think the name was longer, had 'water' in it, didn't it? We were practically the only ones there," he said.

"Like the time your friend loaned us his ski lodge in the middle of summer."

"Yeah, we really were the only ones staying there. A ghost lodge. There's something about those cheap and borrowed places that made it seem like, I don't know, like it would never end. The ritzy places, the Bever— . . . you know, the Hiltons and stuff."

He caught himself, but it was too late. She heard what he started to say. The hotel where he had stayed with that woman, his only—so he claimed—affair. He had almost said it aloud, after all these years. The utterance silenced them both.

"You were thinking about her."

"No, don't be ridiculous—that was over fifteen years ago," he said, trying to remain calm, but she saw his left eye twitch as he poured the remainder of the wine.

"You remember the name of the place you stayed with her, but not the name of the place with me."

"We've stayed in tons of places together. Besides, the place you and I stayed had a Spanish name. The name of the place with her was so common that it just popped into my head. I never think about being with her."

Carol wanted to let it go, but she felt the memory rising inside her, like a flash flood.

"Then why did you start to say it, the name of the hotel?"

"Carol," he said, looking directly into her eyes. "You promised never to bring that up again."

She wanted to say, I didn't, you did; instead, she lifted her glass and twirled the stem between her fingers and thumb.

Though they held hands on their walk back to the hotel, their mood was irrevocably changed. Neither spoke. They passed a girl standing in a doorway wedged between two shops, her key in the lock. Obviously she lived above the stores. Wearing a day-glow green halter top and cut-off jeans, she glanced in their direction as her key clicked. Her eyes were ringed in mascara smudges. Carol smiled at her. Without returning the smile, the girl pushed her shoulder into the door to dislodge it. Carol had an eerie feeling that if she spoke, the girl wouldn't hear. They—she, Stanley, and the girl—were all on the same street, the same place, within touching distance, yet at different times. The girl was in her present, Stanley and Carol in their futures. Carol shivered. The girl disappeared inside.

Their hotel lobby was empty. No one behind the desk. They made the long climb to their room in silence. Upon entering, Stanley strode onto the balcony where the night—illuminated by a three-quarter moon—glowed deep azure. The sky blended so completely with the horizon that he seemed to be suspended in space.

"Have you ever seen so much water?" he asked.

"No," said Carol, coming up behind him. As she reached for him—without plan or forethought—she, instead, grabbed the French doors and pulled them inward, closed. As Stanley turned, she slid the bolt into place. Thinking it a joke, Stanley smiled. The bright moonlight made his translucent ears glow pink. She pulled the sheer curtain across his face and turned away from him.

"Carol, it's not funny," he called, rattling the knob. "Come on, Carol, open the door."

She walked to the bathroom, closed the door, and sat on fuzzy blue cover of the toilet seat where his shouts sounded faint. She doubted anyone else would hear him. The balcony faced the water and they were on the top floor of a practically vacant building. Nor did she think he would break the glass. The panes looked small for his fists. Besides, the wood door panels were too wide for his wrists to snake around.

Rising, she pulled the chain of the bulb above the mirror. The dim light—sixty watts painted blue—made her look young, without wrinkles. She studied her face, as she had years ago, after she had phoned him at the Beverly Hills Hotel. Even fifteen years ago, she was no longer young. Yet that night had been the first time she had thought about aging with pain. Before then, she had always liked her new lines, her scars, as if they were trophies of experience, evidence of living. Even stretch marks made her feel more real. But that night she had become fearful, had realized for the first time that the marks were signs of loss, not gain.

When the cries from outside subsided, Carol turned off the light and returned to the bedroom. She could not see his silhouette through the curtains. She imagined him on the balcony floor resting.

Carol crept to the bed, curled atop the blue spread, and recalled the longest night of her life. She had threatened to leave him if he didn't return by morning. In a rage, she had slammed down the phone, meaning every word. But as the night wore on, her rage had turned to worry, then longing. Pacing the living room, smoking cigarette after cigarette until her mouth tasted of ash, she had darted to the window each time reflections of passing headlights circled the room. Against her wishes, images of Stanley and another woman, naked, limbs tangled, haunted her. Female arms entwined in male arms, hairy legs wrapped around slender, white ones, ribs against ribs. Darkness faded to gray, every item of furnishing bathed in it, then pink. At the sight of him finally pulling in the driveway at sunrise, she had run outside, barefoot, wearing only her robe to greet him. She was ready to forgive him anything. She begged him not to leave her. He promised to stay, and they both promised never to mention the night again.

◈

Carol didn't even know she had fallen asleep until the light woke her. She rose and unlocked the French doors to find Stanley crouched, shivering, against the railing. She offered her hand and pulled him from the void into their room. Walking stiffly, he followed her to the bed. She folded back the blankets and they both slipped beneath.

"It was Casa del Mar Azul," Stanley said, his voice scratchy.

"What?" asked Carol

"That hotel, the one where we stayed on the cliff in Mexico."

"Oh," she said.

Then, like they had for most of their forty-five years together, they curled into one another, like waves overlapping, gently rocking, until sleep claimed them.

Made in the USA
Coppell, TX
09 January 2020